She turned and looked up into the bluest pair of eyes she'd ever seen.

"I kept you wai̇t̲i̇n̲g̲," _____ l. "I'm sorry."

He didn't lo_____ of action. He w_____n-to-the-touch ad_____ll one liked the type.

Abby didn't.

"My daughter and I will both be going on the camping outing—"

He stiffened suddenly, interrupting her. "No way."

"What?" He was dangerously close to looming and she would not be loomed over.

"I won't be nursemaid to a kid."

"Her name is Kimmie, and if the necessity for nursemaiding arises, I'll be the one doing it."

He shook his head. "You don't need me for this. It's overkill. I'll reimburse you."

"I don't want your money. I want my weekend... with you."

Dear Reader,

Whether you're enjoying one of the first snowfalls of the season or lounging in a beach chair at some plush island resort, I hope you've got some great books by your side. I'm especially excited about the Silhouette Romance titles this month as we're kicking off 2006 with two great new miniseries by some of your all-time favorite authors.

Cara Colter teams up with her daughter, Cassidy Caron, to launch our new PERPETUALLY YOURS trilogy. *In Love's Nine Lives* (#1798) a beautiful librarian's extremely possessive tabby tries to thwart a budding romance between *his* mistress and a man who seems all wrong for her but is anything but. Teresa Southwick returns with *That Touch of Pink* (#1799)—the first in her BUY-A-GUY trilogy. When a single mom literally buys a former military man at a bachelor auction to help her daughter earn a wilderness badge, she gets a lot more than she bargained for...and is soon earning points toward *her own* romantic survival badge. Old sparks turn into an all-out blaze when the hero returns to the family ranch in *Sometimes When We Kiss* (#1800) by Linda Goodnight. Finally, Elise Mayr debuts with *The Rancher's Redemption* (#1801) in which a widow, desperate to help her sick daughter, throws herself on the mercy of her commanding brother-in-law whose eyes reflect anything but the hate she'd expected.

And be sure to come back next month for more great reading, with Sandra Paul's distinctive addition to the PERPETUALLY YOURS trilogy and Judy Christenberry's new madcap mystery.

Have a very happy and healthy 2006.

Ann Leslie Tuttle
Associate Senior Editor

Please address questions and book requests to:
Silhouette Reader Service
U.S.: 3010 Walden Ave., P.O. Box 1325, Buffalo, NY 14269
Canadian: P.O. Box 609, Fort Erie, Ont. L2A 5X3

TERESA SOUTHWICK
PRESENTS

THAT TOUCH OF PINK

Buy
-A-
Guy

SILHOUETTE *Romance*®

Published by Silhouette Books

America's Publisher of Contemporary Romance

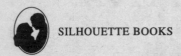 SILHOUETTE BOOKS

ISBN 0-373-19799-3

THAT TOUCH OF PINK

Books by Teresa Southwick

Silhouette Romance

Wedding Rings and Baby Things #1209
The Bachelor's Baby #1233
*A Vow, a Ring, a Baby Swing #1349
The Way to a Cowboy's Heart #1383
*And Then He Kissed Me #1405
*With a Little T.L.C. #1421
The Acquired Bride #1474
*Secret Ingredient: Love #1495
*The Last Marchetti Bachelor #1513
**Crazy for Lovin' You #1529
**This Kiss #1541
**If You Don't Know by Now #1560
**What If We Fall in Love? #1572
Sky Full of Promise #1624
†To Catch a Sheik #1674
†To Kiss a Sheik #1686
†To Wed a Sheik #1696
††Baby, Oh Baby #1704
††Flirting with the Boss #1708
††An Heiress on His Doorstep #1712
§That Touch of Pink #1799

*The Marchetti Family
**Destiny, Texas
†Desert Brides
††If Wishes Were…
§Buy-a-Guy

Silhouette Special Edition

The Summer House #1510
"Courting Cassandra"
Midnight, Moonlight &
  Miracles #1517
It Takes Three #1631
The Beauty Queen's
  Makeover #1699

Silhouette Books

The Fortunes of Texas:
Shotgun Vows

TERESA SOUTHWICK

lives in Southern California with her hero husband who is more than happy to share with her the male point of view. An avid fan of romance novels, she is delighted to be living out her dream of writing for Silhouette Books.

Do you need a man?
The 75ᵀᴴ semiannual
Charity City Auction

Is your chance to find the right one
for that "honey do" list.

Could you use a weekend warrior? Ex-army ranger
Riley Dixon is the guy for you. He's donating a survival
weekend guaranteed to get your heart rate up.

What about that home repair you've been putting off?
Dashing Des O'Donnell, former Charity City High
football hero, now owner and president of his own
construction company, is offering a repair of your choice.

Personal security issues? Defend your honor?
Savvy Sam Brimstone, recently of the LAPD
and a hotshot detective, is your man.

These are just a sampling of the jaw-dropping guys
available to the highest bidder. Ladies, don't miss the
chance to buy a guy—no strings attached.

Cash, Check, Credit and Debit cards gratefully accepted
by the Charity City Philanthropic Foundation.

Prologue

Buy-a-Guy: Semiannual Charity City Auction

Abby Walsh needed a man and she was here to buy the one she wanted.

Many towns held bachelor auctions to raise money. Not hers. Charity City was more creative with its semiannual events. The women's—Sell-A-Belle—was held in the spring. Tonight was the men's turn and bachelorhood wasn't a prerequisite, which was just peachy with Abby. Most of the guys were donating their time and skills to be auctioned because they'd received grants from the town for their businesses or projects. Payback in volunteer form was expected.

The specifics of the sale had been listed ahead of time on the town's Web site and Abby was waiting for the guy who'd donated a survival weekend. Her daughter had recently become involved with a group promoting girls' outdoor activities. Badges were involved and apparently came under the heading "life and death" for her six-year-old. Abby knew if she were in charge of camping, it would be life and death for real. So the auction was the answer to her problem. She could give back to the town and get the perfect guy—for the weekend. She had no illusions about a perfect guy for herself.

She'd rather be alone than need a man for anything. Once had been more than enough.

Normally she attended the annual auctions with her two best girlfriends. Molly Preston was on her right, but Jamie Gibson couldn't make it tonight. Her parents, Louise and Roy Gibson, had come instead.

The Charity City Community Center was the only place in town large enough to house the event, and rows of folding chairs filled the expanse of floor space. On the stage, Mayor Baxter Wentworth was playing auctioneer. Tall, distinguished and gray-haired, he was a descendant of the town's founding family who had initiated the first auction. He took the responsibility of carrying on this charitable tradition very seriously.

"This is Charity City, folks," he said. "We put our money where our mouth is. I don't have to tell you this is the seventy-fifth anniversary of the Buy-A-Guy auction."

"No, you've been reminding us of that for weeks," someone called out.

The mayor laughed along with the rest of the audience. "Okay. I get the point. But you all know the foundation channels money to all of Charity City's worthy causes, and those funds have to come from somewhere.

We're almost finished for tonight and I want to make this the most successful event ever."

After the applause died down, he said, "Okay. We've got three volunteers left. First is a home repair of your choice donated by Des O'Donnell of O'Donnell Construction."

Abby felt an elbow in her ribs and looked at Molly. "What?"

"Bid on that for me."

"Why can't you do it yourself?"

"Don't ask. Just trust me on this. No one can know I'm the one who bought Des." When Abby hesitated, Molly added, "Who would think twice about a single woman buying a home repair?"

"You're a single woman."

Cinnamon-colored eyes assumed a decidedly puppy dog expression. "Yeah. But you're divorced. By definition, that means once upon a time you grew accustomed to a man around the house."

Not her man, Abby thought. He hadn't been around the house all that much. But this was obviously important to her friend and Abby was dead meat when puppy dog eyes were involved. "Okay."

When the mayor announced a starting amount, the bidding began and Abby signaled her interest by raising her number. Apparently she wasn't the only one interested. As other spirited bidders got involved, the price escalated. She slid Molly a questioning look, but her friend simply nodded discreetly.

Finally, everyone else dropped out. The mayor looked around. "Anyone else? Going, going... Sold to the little lady in the third row."

He glanced down at his list. "Our next guy is a visitor to Charity City. Sam Brimstone, a retired LAPD detective. Ellie Campbell, who works over at the Lone Star Bar and Grill, says he's her knight in shining armor, but the judge didn't see it that way. His community service is thirty days to be auctioned off for charity."

He called out a starting bid and Abby was surprised when the Gibsons jumped on it. She couldn't imagine what Jamie's parents wanted with a man busted because he had anger management issues. A determined woman in the back of the room kept up the pressure, but the older couple clearly meant business. Eventually the bids grew too rich for anyone else.

"Going, going," the mayor said, searching the crowd to make sure this was the best he could do. "Gone. Sold to Roy and Louise Gibson."

Abby and Molly exchanged surprised glances that silently asked why the Gibsons wanted a cop. She started to ask when the mayor cleared his throat.

"Our last item is a survival weekend donated by Riley Dixon of Dixon Security. He's a hometown boy, a retired Army Ranger—that's Special Forces for those of you who don't speak military. If anyone's looking for a weekend of thrills and chills, he's just the man who can provide it."

Riley Dixon sounded like Mr. Macho and her worst nightmare. Unfortunately, this was the man she'd come here to buy. She hated that she had to rely on a man for anything. But this wasn't for her; it was for Kimmie.

When the bidding started and she raised her number, whispers commenced around her. She cringed at how needy she must look—buying two men. Why hadn't she thought to ask Molly to return the favor and bid for her? It was too late now. Competition was hot and heavy, but she hung in there and held tough. Every time the amount was increased, she waved her number until, finally, everyone else gave up.

"Going, going, gone." The mayor banged his gavel. "Sold to the little lady in the third row. After you've got that home repair taken care of, you can get away from it all for the weekend." He winked at her. "Thanks for coming, folks. You've done Charity City proud."

Abby got in line to pay and find out how to collect her purchase. Six years ago, she'd needed a man to give her child a name. He'd been a dismal failure. This time, what her child needed wouldn't cost Abby any more than what she'd just paid to buy a guy for the weekend.

Chapter One

Abby Walsh took a deep breath, then punched the Up arrow on the elevator. His office was located in the heart of downtown, taking up an entire floor in one of the city's most prestigious buildings, right across the street from Philanthropy Plaza. With streets named Benevolent Boulevard and Welfare Way, Charity City, Texas, was a place where folks took care of their own.

The money she'd spent at the auction would help fund scholarships, businesses, women's shelters and other worthy causes. That was all well and good, but Abby actually *needed* what Riley Dixon had auctioned. Now it was time to collect.

When the elevator doors whispered open, she stepped inside and sucked in another deep breath. The car went up while her stomach stayed on the main floor. She hated elevators. She hated macho guys. And she hated venturing out of her comfort zone. Hopefully her daughter would appreciate this and the trade-off would be zero rebellion during her teenage years. If *Abby* had done less envelope-pushing and more rule-following, she wouldn't be here now. But she also wouldn't have Kimmie, and she couldn't imagine her life without her child.

When the elevator stopped, Abby stepped out on the top floor into what was the reception area of Dixon Security. An impressive semi-circular cherrywood desk dominated the center of the room, with a sofa and chairs in a grouping off to the side. The thick carpet in a warm, rich shade of beige made her feel as if she were walking on a cloud.

Behind the desk sat a pretty redhead with a nameplate that read Nora Dixon. *Hmm,* Abby thought. He had good taste in women.

"I'm here to see Mr. Dixon."

The woman glanced up, then did a double take. "And you are?" Her tone was on the cool side.

"Abby Walsh. I have an appointment." When the woman checked her computer, she asked, "Do you have me down?"

"Sometimes he writes things on his calendar without bringing it to my attention. Of course, I found out the hard way that I have to cross-reference his calendar with my computer schedule."

"Okay." Abby hadn't talked to him yet. That's why she was here. But far be it from her to butt in when she didn't understand the office's work flow.

The receptionist looked up. "I'm sorry but I *don't* have you down. And he's running late today. You're welcome to wait if that's not a problem?"

Abby looked at her watch. She had to pick up Kimmie from Kid's Klub before six and it was five o'clock now. "I won't take up much of his time."

"I'll let him know you're here." After picking up the phone and announcing Abby, the redhead listened, then waved her to a chair. "He can give you ten minutes."

"That works for me." Abby sat and smoothed her hands over her skirt.

When she was standing, the hem hit her about mid-calf and her sensible, low-heeled shoes only added about an inch and a half to her five feet two inches. Since high-heeled pumps wouldn't add nearly enough height, she settled for practical and comfy instead of willowy and statuesque.

After ten minutes of staring out the window, she glanced at the array of reading material on the end tables. *Military Monthly. Self-Defense.* She wondered where he'd hidden *Guns & Ammo* even as she lamented the absence of *People, Us* or a sleazy gossip magazine with a juicy alien abduction story. She glanced at her watch again and huffed out a breath. He'd given her ten minutes. Unfortunately, he'd been conspicuously absent during that time. She stood and paced the waiting area, glancing at the time every few minutes.

Just when she'd decided she couldn't wait any longer, the door to his office opened and he walked out. "Ms. Walsh?"

She turned away from the window and looked up—way up—into the bluest pair of eyes she'd ever seen. Her stomach, which had finally joined the rest of her on the top floor, plummeted back to square one. In spite of that sensation, she noticed that he looked momentarily startled. Then it was as if invisible shutters closed off his expression.

"The security business must be booming," she said wryly.

"I kept you waiting." His tone was cool; he must have caught it from his receptionist.

"You did."

He folded his arms over a very impressive chest. "I'm sorry."

He didn't look sorry. He looked tall. She estimated about six feet, give or take an inch. His hair was dark, almost black and cut military short, somehow highlighting those amazing eyes. He wore a biceps-hugging navy T-shirt tucked into worn jeans. The ensemble was completed by a pair of scuffed cowboy boots and was by far the most masculine attire she'd ever seen on a businessman. It simply provided evidence that her auction purchase had been the right one.

His nose was slightly off-kilter, and he had a small, thin scar on his square, rugged chin. The battered look suited him. But it also reassured her that he was a man of action. He was also the walking, talking, warm-to-the-touch ad for ruggedly handsome. If one liked the type. She didn't.

He looked at the clock on the wall. "We can talk in my office."

She nodded, then preceded him into the inner sanctum, which turned out to be a stark contrast to the elegant reception area. The only thing that carried over was the thick carpet. Sitting on it was his battered L-shaped desk, which would have looked more at home in a thrift store. But it held what looked like a top-of-the-line computer. Instead of the expensive artwork she'd expected on the walls, they displayed framed photos. She couldn't make out any specific details.

"Have a seat." He indicated one of the utilitarian chrome and gray-blue upholstered chairs in front of the desk. "I have eight minutes."

After he sat behind the desk, she met his gaze. "Your wife said you could give me ten minutes."

"Wife?"

"The receptionist."

"My sister."

Her gaze dropped to his hands. There was no ring on the fourth finger of his left hand. That didn't mean anything. Some married men didn't wear rings. And... And it didn't matter a fig whether he was married.

"Your sister," she said. "So this is a family-owned business?"

"No. I own it. Nora works for me. She's good at her job."

"Meaning if she wasn't, family or not, she'd be canned?"

One broad shoulder lifted in a casual shrug. "Yeah."

"Do you have a wife?" Doggone it. She hadn't meant to ask that. She didn't care. But the rogue part of her subconscious that had temporarily taken over her brain neglected to send that message to her mouth.

"I'm not married." His gaze was penetrating as he frowned at her. "Now you've got six minutes. And if my marital status has something to do with why you're here, you're wasting my time. I can put those six minutes to better use."

"Look, I'm a people person. That makes me curious.

It was certainly not my intention to offend you with the question."

His impassive look gave no clue to what he was thinking. "So you have a security concern?"

Wow. He gave the expression *single-minded determination* a run for its money. Not to mention that his tone was just this side of abrasive. "Apparently in your line of work, one can be successful even without courtesy and charm."

"If you're here about personal safety, home or business protection, I can be as charming and courteous as the next guy. If not…"

"I'm here because I bought the survival weekend you donated to the Charity City auction. I mentioned that to whoever I spoke with on the phone."

It seemed impossible, but his frown deepened. "I didn't get the message."

"And I didn't actually get an appointment. Is your sister's job in jeopardy?"

"No. She was sick recently. A temp replaced her."

His shoulders shifted almost imperceptibly as his mouth straightened into a thin line, telling her he was disapproving. She'd known him about two and a half minutes—although he was the only one keeping exact time—so how she knew he was surprised or annoyed, she couldn't say. But she'd stake her reputation as Charity City High School's favorite librarian that he was both surprised *and* annoyed.

"So you're the one who bought the survival weekend?" He sounded skeptical.

She nodded. "And I'm here to make arrangements to collect it."

He let his gaze drop to her cap-sleeved silk shell with the loose-fitting floral jumper over it. "Why?"

"Because I paid for it."

He shook his head. "Why did you buy it in the first place?"

"Correct me if I'm wrong, but I don't believe part of the deal is explaining my motivation."

"You don't look like the outdoorsy type."

The fact that he was right made her resent his attitude even more. "If we're judging books by covers, Mr. Dixon, you don't look like the type, either."

"What type would that be?"

"One who would donate to charity. The type to give back to his community."

"It was a debt."

"Oh?"

"The foundation gave me interest free start-up capital for my business."

"And when one benefits from the auction proceeds, one is obligated to give back."

"I always pay my debts," he confirmed.

"Very reassuring. That's why I'm here. My daughter, Kimmie, belongs to The Bluebonnets—"

"What?"

"It's an organization that sponsors outdoor activities for girls in her age group—"

"How old?"

"Excuse me?"

What did that have to do with sleeping outside and starting a fire with two sticks when she was on a very tight schedule? She'd be wasting less of her remaining time if he would impart information in sentences of more than three two-syllable words. And she had no il-lusions. When the allotted time was up, he *would* throw her out. She stole a glance at his biceps, the intriguing place where the sleeve of his T-shirt clung to the bulg-ing muscle. There was no doubt in her mind that if he wanted her out, he would and could pick her up bodily and make it so.

"How old is your daughter?"

"Six. When I saw the weekend listed for auction, I knew it was exactly what I needed. And I figured I could kill two birds with one stone."

"Oh?"

"Yes." Maybe he was finally listening and they could wrap this up quickly. "I could do my civic duty in sup-port of the town charity. Buying your services to get my daughter her hiking and nature badges—"

"You can't take her camping?"

"I could," she said. "But her survival might be in question. I'm afraid you were right about me. My idea of the outdoors involves a lounge chair, a pool and a sissy drink with an umbrella in it."

"What about your husband?"

Now who was digging for personal info? Although she had to admit Riley had a better reason. It was a log-ical question. "I don't have a husband."

Not any more. And she couldn't be happier. She was glad she no longer had to rely on flaky Fred Walsh. As an unwed pregnant teenager whose baby needed a father, she'd seriously relied on him. If only she could blame it on pressure from her parents. But they'd made it clear they would support her decisions. As it turned out, the decision she'd made hadn't been worthy of support.

"So you're going to dump the kid on me for the weekend?"

"Of course not. Do I look like the kind of mother who would turn her child over to a complete stranger? The two of us will be going on the outing—"

He stood suddenly, interrupting her. "No way."

She blinked. "What?"

"I said no. It's a survival weekend."

"I'm aware of that." She got to her feet. He was dangerously close to looming and she would not be loomed over.

"I won't be nursemaid to a kid."

"Her name is Kimmie. And she needs her two badges. If the necessity for nursemaiding arises, I'll be the one doing it."

He shook his head. "You don't need me for this. It's overkill."

"Maybe. But I've already paid for you."

"I'll reimburse you."

"I don't want your money. I want my weekend."

"No."

"I want you to sue him, the foundation, Mayor Wentworth, the rest of his family, every person he's ever known and anyone else I can think of." Abby paced the length of her small living room.

She loved the fifteen hundred square feet of space she'd purchased six months ago. Unfortunately when she was this angry, the state of Texas wasn't big enough for the amount of pacing she needed to do. Fortunately, her daughter was upstairs in her room playing with her dolls and wasn't watching her mother's display of temper.

"Suing the whole town is a little extreme, don't you think?" Jamie Gibson asked.

Abby had called Jamie right after leaving Dixon Security and they'd met here at the house. She was the attorney who'd handled Abby's divorce two years ago. They'd become friends in spite of the fact that Abby envied her brunette curls, which were the polar opposite of her own stick-straight brown hair. And Jamie was beautiful, a fact the attorney didn't seem to care about. She poured her energy into building a legal career based on integrity, intelligence, and unflagging client support. But Abby felt there was some serious flagging in her attorney's support on the Riley Dixon issue. And how the heck could Jamie sit so calmly on that overstuffed pink floral sofa when there was some heavy-duty suing to be done?

"The man is a welsher," Abby cried, hands on hips as she stared at the bemused, indulgent expression on her friend's face.

"We haven't established all the facts yet. The way I understand it, he escorted you out of his office after he said no. If he is, in fact a welsher, at least he's a gentleman welsher."

"I paid for the weekend he donated to the auction. The check cleared already. And he's refusing to make good on the deal. Maybe you'd prefer Indian giver?"

"Native American would be a little more politically correct," Jamie pointed out.

"Politically correct would be for him to give me what I paid for—a weekend campout so Kimmie can earn her nature badges. I should have seen this coming. After all, he's a man. By definition, that makes him a slacker."

"Are we talking about Riley Dixon or your ex-husband?"

"They're interchangeable," Abby said.

"Is he as hot as I've heard?"

"Who? Fred?"

"I've seen Fred," Jamie pointed out. "I meant Dixon."

"He wouldn't have to wear a bag over his head in public," she grudgingly admitted.

An image of the man's dark hair, blue eyes and flawless physique flashed through her mind and Abby braced herself as her stomach lurched from the same elevator sensation she'd experienced just a short while ago. But, he was a reminder about judging a book by its cover—a hunk with the face of a hero and the heart of a welsher.

"So he's really good-looking?" Jamie pushed, obviously wanting details.

"He's weathered," she said carefully. "A little bent and battered, but buff in all the right places."

"So you like him," Jamie declared in a grating I-knew-it tone.

"I don't like him. But I'm not blind and I don't tell lies in spite of the fact I don't like him. Here's the thing. When he told me he wouldn't take us on the campout, I got that Fred-feeling in my gut."

"You're telling me Dixon is a shallow jerk who'd leave you in the lurch to try out for a TV reality show?"

"It's not the trying-out part. It's the finding-Ms.-*Fear-Factor*-who-jumped-on-his-bandwagon-and-his-bones-after-which-he-never-came-back part," Abby said, remembering that particular brand of devastation. "And I don't know if Dixon would do that. I never intend to find out. Because in my book, breaking one's word on first acquaintance is a giant red flag."

"From what I've heard, Riley Dixon is a hard worker. A former Army Ranger who's built a profitable security business in under five years. Soldiers don't get to be Rangers by slacking off."

"Then we're back to welsher." She met her friend's gaze and sighed. "Okay. I'll admit to some lingering hostility toward the man who shirked most of his responsibilities—the most important one being his daughter."

"I understand why you'd have this over-the-top reaction. Kimmie doesn't have a dad, and you've got to be both mother and father to her."

"That's all true. But I've come to terms with it." She ignored her friend's raised eyebrow. "Part of coming to terms with it is knowing my limitations. I bought Riley Dixon to fulfill the father role for the weekend. How was I to know that he's a macho jerk who breaks his promises? In my book, that makes him a Fred The Flake clone." Abby huffed out a breath that lifted her bangs off her forehead. "Like all men, Riley Dixon is ducking his obligations."

"Not all men are that way."

"No? Couldn't prove it by me."

"Let me rephrase. Not all men are flakes. Just the ones you meet."

"Why is that? I'm a high school librarian. Every day I deal with kids who don't return books, don't turn in assignments and just generally don't do what they're supposed to do. It's my job to mold them into capable, dependable, efficient, honest adults. Admittedly, I've only been doing this for a little over three years, but I've had students come back and say I've made a difference in their lives. So is it just bad karma that I'm surrounded by irresponsible, dishonest men? Am I a flake magnet? Should I roll over and let Mr. Macho walk all over me? What recourse do generally law-abiding people have when someone doesn't live up to their obligation?"

"Did you or did you not say he offered to reimburse you?"

"He did."

"So take the money and hire one of those mounted police guys. I hear they're quite impressive in their tight trousers and red coats. The hats are a little funny-looking, though."

One corner of Abby's mouth twitched in amusement. "Texas is a little far from the Canadian border to make that a viable solution."

"Too bad," Jamie sighed. "What about a Texas Ranger? The hats are better, and they're right in our own backyard."

"That's law enforcement, not nature guide."

"They're hot, too."

Abby stared at her. "Maybe you need to go home and take a cold shower."

"I don't want to go home," she said, an odd look on her face.

Instantly alert, Abby stopped pacing. "Is something wrong, Jamie?"

"No." She shrugged.

"Do you want to talk about it?" Abby asked. "Does it have anything to do with the guy your parents bought you at the auction?"

A smile curved up the corners of Jamie's mouth. "Yeah. A little. I'm dealing with it. No big deal."

Abby had learned that if her friend didn't want to talk about something, nothing could drag it out of her. So they might as well go back to the problem at hand. "Okay. Let's come up with some really creative grounds for suing Riley Dixon." Abby was glad when her words produced a laugh.

"So you refuse to let him reimburse you and just camp out with Kimmie in your new backyard and take her to the park for a walk?"

"No can do," Abby said. "Not authentic enough for The Bluebonnets. It's gotta be real. At least one night living off the land. With dirt and no flushing toilets. Microwave bad, fire good," she said in her best caveman voice.

Jamie laughed. "That seems pretty extreme."

"Don't tell Kimmie that. She's got her heart set on getting all her badges. You know her. When she gets something in her head, she's going to do it. And come hell or high water, she'll get it perfect. I keep telling myself that determination is a good quality in an adult."

"There's got to be another way."

"I don't want to find another way. I had it all figured out and paid for." She held her hands out, palms up. A helpless gesture, and she hated feeling helpless—maybe even more than she hated relying on a man. "What am I going to do?"

"Talk to him again." Jamie shrugged as if it were that easy.

"Are you saying you won't sue him?"

"No. I'm saying people are too sue-happy these days when a simple conversation could save time, aggravation and money. He's ex-military. Surely he's a rational, logical man."

Abby sighed. "Listen to yourself. Any self-respecting legal eagle would take this case and run with it for all the billable hours they could get. You, my friend, are going to starve."

"I can afford to take off a few pounds."

"You are so lying. And you're too thin. You're sure there's nothing you want to talk about?"

"No. Except I know you don't really want to sue Riley Dixon. You just needed to let off steam."

"Busted," Abby said.

"And I suspect the name-calling did wonders for your anger abatement level."

"You think slacker, welsher, jerk and flake helped?"

"I do, indeed."

Abby sighed. "You'd be right. But don't let on to Kimmie. I always tell her to use people's given names and I'm fairly certain none of the above are on Fred's birth certificate. Or Dixon's, either, for that matter."

"She'll never hear it from me. But in that spirit, I'd be happy to role-play with you for your next conversation with Riley Dixon."

The thought of seeing him again sent quivers through Abby and she remembered the mayor's comment on auction night about thrills and chills. His words were turning out to be annoyingly prophetic. She wondered if she might be better off if she waved the white flag and retreated.

Riley Dixon watched the elevator doors close, then turned to his sister. "We got the contract."

Nora smiled. "To put security systems in all the district's high schools?"

"Yup. Starting with Charity City High."

"Congratulations."

"Yeah."

"So you're excited?" Nora asked, toying with the pen on her desk.

"Of course."

"Then why do you look like someone let your favorite pistol rust in the rain?"

"I don't know." He ran his fingers through his hair. "I guess it's because we shouldn't need metal detectors and surveillance systems in high schools."

"It doesn't mean that all kids have gone over to the dark side," she pointed out.

"I know."

"You can't take responsibility for what's wrong with the world today."

"I know that, too. But it seems wrong to profit from it."

She lifted her shoulders. "The Board of Education budgeted for the security measures. And frankly, if they've decided it's necessary, I'll sleep better at night knowing they've hired the best company for the job. So will a lot of high school parents. Mostly the kids are good, normal kids. You've been hired to make sure they're safe from the occasional bad apple. The school district feels it's money well spent. Why don't you?"

"Thanks for trying to make me feel better."

"You're welcome. In exchange, I'd like to know why you practically threw Abby Walsh out of your office." She tucked a strand of auburn hair behind her ear and met his gaze.

Riley knew his sister well, meaning she wasn't going to back off. "She was here to make arrangements for the survival weekend I donated to the Charity City auction."

"Wow. That clears up any confusion," she said sarcastically. "And here I thought she'd done something really bad. Like having the audacity to look a lot like Barb Kelly."

Riley winced. Abby Walsh was petite and feminine and beautiful. Her skin looked soft and her shiny brown hair even softer. It was like a curtain of silk teasing her shoulders. And Nora was right. Abby looked an awful lot like the pregnant woman he'd married to give her baby a name. The same woman who walked out two years later when the biological father finally showed up to claim his rights. Better late than never had made him feel like hell.

"Her daughter needs some kind of scouting badges," he explained.

"And you jumped to the conclusion that she was cut from Barb Kelly cloth and dumping the kid on you."

"Yeah." Just like old times, he thought. "I'm glad you understand." It's what he loved about Nora.

"But I don't understand. Didn't you clarify the situation?"

He sat in one of the chairs in front of her desk. "She claimed she'd never turn the kid over to a complete stranger and said she'd be going on the `outing' too." He huffed out a breath. "Outing. As if it's a society picnic with hoity-toity baskets and buckets of champagne."

"It couldn't be possible that you thought she was phat."

"You've got eyes. Did you think she was overweight?"

He thought she had the curviest little body he'd seen

in a long time, although it was hard to tell in that full-skirted thing she'd been wearing. But her arms were toned and the silky shirt she wore under it molded to her breasts in a way that tempted a man and made him hot all over.

"I didn't say F-A-T. I said P-H-A-T—pretty hot and tempting."

"No," he lied. "I didn't think that."

"Okay. Then I have to conclude you're scared."

He stood, to crank up the intimidation factor, and glared down at her. "This is me we're talking about. When I was in the army, I parachuted into hostile territory with nothing but a knife, a sidearm and a radio. I'm not afraid of anything."

"And this is me," Nora said, unfazed by the intimidation ploy. "I was there to pick up the pieces when Barb Kelly walked out with the child you fell in love with—"

"Don't go there," he warned.

"Why not? You just did."

"No, not where you think. I just faced reality a long time ago. I'm a place-holder."

"Not that again." She sighed. "Poor you. You were adopted, and Mom and Dad love me best because I have their DNA. Trust me, it's not that special."

"You're wrong. You're pretty special."

"So are you. For the record—and this is the last time I'm inflating your fragile male ego—the folks love you. Dad's shirt buttons are in serious jeopardy of popping every time he boasts to his buddies about his son the Army Ranger."

"Enough," he said. "I'm not a kid any more."

"You're acting like one."

"Am not." He grinned as she sighed. "Do me a favor and just bury it."

"You can duck into your foxhole if you want," she said. "But I think you noticed the resemblance to Barb, too, and it scared the stuffing out of you."

"You'd be wrong."

"Then why did you refuse to keep your word and do the survival weekend?"

"I'm busy. Just got the new contract."

"You didn't have it in the bag when she was here. Definitely scared."

"Busy."

"Scared."

"Busy." Now it was his turn to sigh.

Squabbling just like when they were kids. And their parents had always seemed to take her side. Because she was their biological child and he'd been adopted when they'd thought conceiving their own baby was impossible. But there was something about Nora. He simply couldn't hold it against her that she was a product of the folks' love and DNA. He'd felt protective of her from the moment she had come home from the hospital. He had a bond with her. More than that—he loved her.

"Is there any way I can convince you you're wrong?" he asked.

"Yes."

"Are you going to share, or do I have to use more aggressive interrogation techniques?"

"No tickling," she warned.

"Then talk."

"Right back at you, Riley. Face Abby Walsh. And talk." She sighed at his look. "The thing is, you don't have a choice. This is you. Although you try to hide all your good qualities behind a surly exterior, I happen to know you're loyal, honest and you always pay your debts and do your duty. You gave your word to the Charity City Foundation when you volunteered the weekend for auction. And you're an honorable man. You can't do anything *but* talk to her."

He hated that she was right. "Okay. You win."

"Good." She pointed at him. "But remember. That doesn't mean the talk needs to be personal. In fact, if I were you, I wouldn't under any circumstances get involved with her."

"You're preaching to the choir, sis. I don't do personal. I'll smooth things over." Things like the curve of her cheek and the slender column of her neck. The insubordinate thoughts made him grind his teeth and proved that Abby Walsh was trouble with a capital T. "By the time I'm finished oozing charm, she'll be glad to let me compensate her for the money she spent."

And he'd be off one very large, very uncomfortable hook.

Chapter Two

A half hour after deciding to be sweet and lovable in his quest to change Abby Walsh's mind, Riley stood on her doorstep. He'd have been there sooner, but it took him a few minutes to find out where she lived.

Her place was in The Villas, one of Charity City's newest areas built by Richmond Homes. It was a charming neighborhood, meaning he was in the right place to take his charm out for a spin and see what it could do. And she'd accused him of *lacking* charm and courtesy. She was in for the charmfest of her life, he thought, pushing the doorbell.

"Who's there?" It was a child's voice behind the door.

"Riley Dixon," he answered.

"The man Mommy bought at the auction?"

"Yes." His reputation preceded him.

The door opened and a pint-size girl stood in front of him wearing pink satin pajamas, matching slippers with feathers on the toes and a pink robe with cartoon princesses on it. Her hair was long enough to disappear behind her shoulders, but what he could see of it was wet. Taking a mental leap, he guessed she'd just had her evening bath and was dressed for bed.

"Kimmie?" he said, remembering how Abby had corrected him when he'd called her "the kid."

"Yes."

He noticed the sleeves and hem of her robe were trimmed with white lace and tried to picture her camping in rugged terrain. Paying back the Charity City foundation should have been easy. Take a guy camping and teach him a few survival skills. End of obligation. But his luck wasn't that good. The woman who'd bought him would consider a broken nail a life-altering event. And her child no doubt took after her.

"I'd like to talk to your mom. Is she here?"

There was a ten-year-old car in the driveway, but that didn't mean the mom in question was on the premises.

"Mommy's in the attic. It's upstairs, and the ladder is pulled down." She glanced over her shoulder. "I'm watchin' TV before I hafta go to bed and I don't have a lot of time."

"It's okay. I can find her."

After Kimmie went back to her show, he looked around. Abby's place was small, but very nice. And very pink. It was like living in a Pepto-Bismol bottle. Everything he'd seen so far confirmed his decision to return her money. Shaking his head, he climbed the stairs and found the attic access just as Kimmie had said. As he got closer to the ceiling opening, there was the distinct scraping sound of boxes being moved followed by a lot of grunting and panting.

Riley poked his head through the opening and noticed the attic was crudely finished, with a wooden floor and unpainted wallboard. Obviously she used it for storage, but judging by the boxes stacked against the walls and so high over her head she couldn't reach them, he figured she hadn't put them there. She'd said she didn't have a husband. But that didn't rule out boyfriends.

In sweatpants and a white T-shirt, a barefoot Abby stood with her back to him. Without the flowing skirt, he could see for himself that she was as curvy as he'd guessed. Before he could shut down the thought, he realized he was glad she wasn't wearing jeans that would compress her softness into stiff denim. Quickly he clamped the lid on that image even as his palms tingled at the idea of touching her.

She reached up for a box and maneuvered it forward, then staggered under the weight. He moved quickly to take it from her and when she saw him, she jumped back with a screech of surprise.

She pressed her hand to her heaving chest. "What are you doing here? How did you know where I live?"

"It's my business. I'm in security."

"Funny how that doesn't make me feel secure."

Ignoring her verbal projectile, he said, "Kimmie let me in."

She rubbed a finger beneath her nose. "I guess I need to give her a refresher course in stranger danger."

"I'm not a danger. Besides, she asked who was at the door."

"Because she's not tall enough to see through the peephole."

"Are you?" He gauged her height. "Tall enough to see out of it, I mean."

"I think it was installed by the Jolly Green Giant. But that's beside the point and doesn't explain what you're doing here."

"I wanted to talk to you, Ms. Walsh. To apologize for my behavior earlier."

"Oh?" She fixed him with a skeptical look as she folded her arms beneath her breasts.

Her stance did interesting things to her chest and he had to regroup to remember why he was there. Charm. Yeah. That was it. "I may have been a little abrupt—"

"May have been? Abrupt? Buster, you could give lessons."

"Okay. I deserve that. And I'm here to say I'm sorry." He watched her face, waiting for a sign that his charm was working. A second later, her mouth softened and a small smile set off her dimples. He wondered how many men she'd brought to their knees with them.

"I accept your apology, Mr. Dixon."

"Riley," he said.

"And I'm Abby. As opposed to Ms. Walsh."

"Okay. Look, I wanted to talk to you about the survival weekend."

"Actually if you hadn't stopped by tonight, I was going to drop in at your office tomorrow to discuss it."

"Great minds," he said, referring to thinking alike.

"Yeah." She rested her hands on her hips. "You first. What did you want to say?"

"First, may I say what a lovely daughter you have."

Her face brightened at the words. "Thank you. I think she's pretty special."

"And very pretty, too. The pink satin princess thing works for her."

"Yeah. She likes to take her bath early and watch television before bed. The pajamas and robe are her favorites and—"

"Not warm enough for camping."

The expression of benevolence disappeared, replaced by skepticism. "I wouldn't let her wear them camping."

"It's not just the sleepwear. Camping is an all-or-nothing sort of thing. You admitted it's not your cup of tea," he pointed out, recalling her remark about pools and sissy drinks.

The sweats were good, but he'd give a lot to see her in a bikini by that pool, and maybe wet… Damn, he was going to have to get his thoughts under control or he was dead in the water. Nora was right. There was a striking physical resemblance between Abby and his ex-wife. But, now that the shock had worn off, he could see the differences. Abby's eyes were brown, a warm rich shade of cocoa, and there was a sweetness about her Barb had never possessed. But there were similarities, too, like they both needed him. Different reasons, but Abby still wanted something from him. He needed to get out of this ASAP.

"The outdoors isn't my cup of tea," she confirmed. "But Kimmie wants her hiking and camping badges. I figured a survival weekend would kill two birds with one stone—maximize my auction purchase. It's only one night. I can suck it up."

"You think so? Without hot showers, or cold, for that matter, since there won't be running water. Dirt is a major component. The ground is hard and damn cold.

TV is out of the question. No electricity," he explained. "It's dark and Mother Nature didn't think to install street lights. Not a whole lot to do but sit around and watch the leaves fall. No froufrou food or microwaves."

"Because there's no electricity?" she asked sweetly, too sweetly.

"Even if there was, a microwave would be too bulky and heavy to backpack in. Only necessities get lugged over rugged terrain." He planted his feet wide apart and rested his hands on his hips as he stared down at her. "It's primitive and uncomfortable. So you see—"

"No." She started to walk by him.

He stopped her with a hand on her arm. "Wait a minute. What does that mean?"

"You should know. It's what you told me a little while ago. What part of 'no' don't *you* understand?"

"I know what it means. Are you saying you got the message that camping isn't for you and you'll let me reimburse you—with interest—for what you paid at the auction?"

"And let you off the hook?"

"A man can hope."

"Not a chance." She took a step toward him, close enough that their bodies were nearly touching and the subtle, sexy fragrance of her perfume filled his head and fogged his brain. "I understand that you weren't expecting Kimmie and I when you donated the weekend campout. But we're what you got. And now you're stuck with us. If you're going to fulfill your obligation to the foundation, you need to suck it up and get over whatever prejudice you've got against—"

"It's okay, Mommy."

Abby whirled away from him at the sound of her daughter's voice. The little girl was sitting cross-legged, with her feminine little robe tucked around her, just inside the attic opening. Riley didn't have a clue how long she'd been there. Not good for a man who'd at one time prided himself on being able to hear a leaf drop when his life depended on it. And for reasons he didn't want to think about, he was feeling as if his life depended on making this stubborn woman understand why he couldn't do what he'd promised.

Abby went to her child and squatted next to her. "What's okay, sweetie?"

"If he doesn't want to take us on the campout, it's all right."

"I know how much you want your survival badges, Kimmie."

"I did, but—" The little girl shrugged.

"You know if you don't get both of these badges in the next six weeks, you can't go on to the next level in The Bluebonnets."

"I know."

"And Caitlyn will be going on ahead of you into a more advanced group with a different leader. Remember she's getting her last badge at the next meeting?"

The little girl nodded. "But it's okay. Grandma told me that disappointment is part of life. And growing up means learning to live with it."

"I let you down. Sweetie, I'm so sorry—" Abby's voice broke.

"It's not you, Mommy. If my daddy had come back like he promised, he'd have taken me camping. But he stayed in California. I'm six now. I'm big enough to understand."

"I wish I was," Abby mumbled. "Why did you come up here? Did you need something?"

"You need to tuck me in. It's time for bed." Her voice broke on the last word and her chin started quivering just before she disappeared through the opening.

Riley felt like pond scum. Slimier than pond scum. Both of them were close to tears. Damn it to hell. If he agreed, he would have to hang with Abby overnight. That was a bad idea, outdoors or anywhere else. And if it was just her, he could have stuck to his guns and pulled out of the op. In the Rangers, he'd worked and trained and prided himself on being the toughest of the tough. But nothing had hardened him enough to say no to a six-year-old who'd already gotten a bum deal.

Charm was no match for a little girl's tears.

"Okay."

"What?" Abby turned her big brown eyes on him.

If he hadn't already caved, he'd be in danger now. "I'll take you and Kimmie camping."

She blinked, then the corners of her mouth curved into a brilliant smile that turned her killer dimples loose on him. She threw herself against him and wrapped her arms around his neck. "Thank you. Thank you. Thank you."

She felt way too good, soft in all the right places and he was relieved when she pulled away.

"What do we need to bring?"

He ran his hand through his hair. "I'll bring the equipment. You and Kim be ready at six a.m. on Saturday morning."

"Aye, aye, sir."

"That's Navy. Yes, sir, will suffice."

"Yes, sir. Whatever you say, sir," she said, brown eyes shining.

That look backed him up a step. It was the same one she'd had just before throwing her arms around him. He wanted her to do it again; at the same time, he knew it was a very bad idea. Because if she ever hugged him again, he knew he'd really get into it. He'd pull her as close as he could get her and press his mouth to hers.

Bad didn't begin to describe this situation. He just hoped he didn't regret this decision.

Abby glanced at Riley's impassive face and wished she knew what he was thinking. Scratch that. It would probably be better if she didn't know. She watched a sleepy Kimmie play with the soggy cocoa cereal in her bowl. They were already behind schedule because Riley had spent ten minutes disapproving of their attire. Capris were bad— legs need to be covered in heavy-duty material to prevent scratches and bug bites. They'd changed into jeans. Their shoes were an accident waiting to happen—sandals gave no support or protection. They'd changed again.

She watched him watch Kimmie. "If I'd known there was a dress code, I would have followed it."

His gaze swung to hers. "Noted."

"Okay, Kim, I think you're finished," she said, sliding the bowl off the table and carrying it to the sink. As quickly as possible, she dumped the remaining light brown milk and cereal, ran the disposal, then put the dirty dishes in the dishwasher. "We've already disrupted Mr. Dixon's schedule."

"It makes good sense to set up camp in the daylight," he said.

His delivery was so smooth, Abby almost missed the subtle sarcasm. "Then we'd better get a move on."

Kim rested her cheek in her palm. "I'm sleepy, Mommy."

"I know, sweetie. But you can sleep in Mr. Dixon's car on the drive." She looked at Riley. "That's okay, isn't it?"

"Sure."

The little girl hopped off her chair and grabbed the box of cereal that was almost as big as she was. "I'll take these for a snack later."

Riley took a step away from the doorway where he'd been standing for the last ten minutes. "That's a negative on the cereal."

She blinked up at him. "Does that mean no?"

"It does."

"But why?"

"Because it's empty calories."

"Huh?" she said, scratching her head.

"It won't maintain your energy level. Besides," he continued, "we're hiking in to where we're going to camp. That box is too bulky and we have more important things to carry."

"Apparently my cosmetics weigh a ton," Abby said, lamenting the little makeup bag she'd been ordered to leave behind.

One corner of his mouth curved up when his gaze met hers. "That's not essential."

"That's a matter of opinion." Thank goodness she'd remembered the lack of electricity and left out her blow-dryer and hot rollers. The humiliation would have been too much.

"You're lucky I let you talk me into that cream stuff."

"Thank goodness my moisturizer has an SPF fifteen."

"To protect your skin." His voice turned gruff. "But the rule is if you can't eat it or use it for shelter, it's not a necessity."

"I eat chocolate cereal," Kimmie said hopefully.

He looked at her. "The benefit doesn't outweigh the negative."

"This is where I remind you that The Bluebonnets only require us to spend one night living off the land. It's okay to relax your standards for us civilians."

"Relaxing standards can compromise a mission. After we hike to the campsite you'll thank me."

Kimmie looked up at him. "But the box isn't heavy."

Abby took pity on him. "I appreciate that you're trying to explain things to her. But sometimes a unilateral no is the best course of action."

His gaze narrowed. "Whatever you say. I don't know much about kids."

"That almost makes us even. I know zero about camping. Which is why I need you—" That didn't sound right. She didn't need him. Any beefy, brainless, no-neck outdoorsman would do. But he was none of those things. In fact, he had a nice, strong-looking neck and she would like to press her lips to a spot... Not going there, she thought. "I mean the great outdoors is why I bought you— Hired your services— So to speak."

"I get it."

While they talked, Kimmie started out of the kitchen with the cereal box under her arm and Abby grabbed it. "Not so fast, young lady. This stays here. Riley said no."

Kimmie looked up as she scuffed the toe of her new pink sneaker on the tile floor. "What if I get hungry?"

"I'm sure Mr. Dixon has that situation under control."

Abby shuddered to think what that meant. Dehydrated meals, beef jerky, energy bars hard as hockey pucks that also served as lethal weapons. As her anxiety level spiked, she reminded herself that it was one night. And she could afford to lose a couple of pounds. Every cloud had a silver lining, and she tried desperately to find it in this situation.

She glanced at Riley's face as he watched Kimmie pick up her princess backpack. She found another silver lining in his expression, which bordered on horror. When he'd agreed to take them on the trip, she knew it was because of what Kimmie had said about disappointment. She'd watched him melt like a chocolate bar left out in the sun. That Riley would be a challenge to resist. But this Riley…his tight lips and narrowed eyes told her the bullheaded bozo was back. Resisting him would be a piece of cake.

Bring on the great outdoors, she thought happily.

Why had she ever thought that hiring an expert would make this easy? She'd left the location of the campsite up to him, but apparently she'd neglected to mention that he needed to take into account Kimmie's age and physical limitations. The Bluebonnets weren't unreasonable in their badge expectations, but she'd bought Rambo.

They'd walked for what seemed like days. Even after numerous stops to rest, they were exhausted. When Riley glanced over his shoulder to study them, he obviously decided they looked like something the cat choked up because he stopped for a rest. Again.

Abby and Kimmie practically collapsed on a prone log. He'd carried most of the equipment on an aluminum frame strapped to his back and looked ready to pose for the cover of *Great Outdoors* magazine. She and Kimmie only had their backpacks with one day's clothing and looked like they'd been lost in the woods for a week. Thank goodness he'd confiscated the cereal box. But she was still bitter about her makeup.

After resting for a few minutes, she noticed the wind had kicked up and clouds were rolling in.

Riley frowned as he studied the sky. "There's still a way to go yet, and we need daylight to set up camp. Shelter could be a priority. We need to get a move on."

Abby wished for his impassive look to replace his current expression. Something told her he didn't scare easily and that his frown was panic for anyone else. This was a heck of a time to get the meaning of "be careful what you wish for." She'd gotten her wish, which meant they were stuck out in the middle of nowhere and taking orders from Rambo—good-looking though he might be here in his element. To make matters worse, that made her want to look her best. Which put taking a bath at the top of her priority list.

And washing her hair—it was limp and stringy because she was sweaty and dirty. After she bathed, she wanted to put on makeup and blow-dry her hair. But she couldn't do any of that because her necessities were at home. And how shallow was she to be thinking about any of that, what with the wind kicking up.

"Abby," he barked out. "Let's get going."

"Yes, sir," she said, standing on shaky legs and saluting.

"Very funny." But in his eyes there was a spark of what appeared to be genuine amusement.

She looked at the dark clouds. "It looks like a storm's moving in. But I checked the weather."

"Me, too. It was supposed to be clear and mild," he said. "I guess this is a rogue. We need to hurry."

Kimmie stood beside her and slid her hand around Abby's waist. "I can't go fast. My new shoes hurt."

Abby pulled off her daughter's socks and shoes and saw she had blisters on both feet. "Why didn't you say something, sweetie?"

"It wasn't so bad." She looked at the sky as she brushed away the hair that had blown into her mouth. "Is there gonna be thunder?"

"Maybe," he said, resting his hands on lean hips.

"I don't like thunder," she said. "Sometimes there's tornadoes when there's thunder."

"Not always." Abby tucked a strand of hair behind her daughter's ear. In seconds, the wind had blown it free. She wasn't into predicting weather, but it seemed as if it was getting darker.

"But sometimes," Kimmie said, "we go to our safe room when the wind gets really bad."

"That's right."

Kimmie looked up at her with a trusting expression on her face. "Do tents have safe rooms?"

Abby glanced at the compactly compressed wad of nylon on Riley's backpack. "Good question, kiddo. Riley?"

He stopped studying the clouds and met her gaze. "Yeah?"

"What happens if things get worse?"

"These blow up suddenly and are gone just as fast. But I'd feel better if we had camp set up. We can bandage those blisters and she'll be good to go."

Kimmie clung to her and started sniffling. "Mommy, I'm scared."

"It's okay, honey. We'll be all right. Riley knows what he's doing."

"But he can't make the storm go away," her daughter pointed out.

As if to give her statement an exclamation point, the echo of rumbling thunder drifted to them.

"Mommy?"

"I know, sweetie." Abby patted her daughter's back as the child buried her face in her shirt. "Riley, do you think this is a good idea? Do you think we should stay out in the open?"

He squatted down in front of them, his forearm resting on his thigh. In spite of her mounting anxiety, Abby noticed the way the denim pulled across the muscles in his leg.

"That storm is at least ten miles away. Unless the wind changes, it will miss us by a lot." He looked at Kimmie. "In frontier days, they didn't have houses as strong as we do now," he pointed out. "And they survived. Isn't that what The Bluebonnets is all about? Seeing how the pioneers lived? Survival under adverse conditions?"

"Yeah. Survival is the key thing here," Abby agreed. "And that wind is making me question survival. What if there is a t-o-r-n-a-d-o?"

Kimmie was pretty bright, but Abby didn't think she could spell that yet. Deliberately, she kept her voice neutral instead of letting it shoot up an octave into a shriek the way she wanted. Kimmie was quivering against her and Abby didn't want to lose her composure and scare her daughter even more than she already was.

Riley smiled. The man had the audacity—or maybe it was the insanity—to look completely unconcerned. "The last time I checked, Texas is pretty big. The odds of a t-o-r-n-a-d-o landing on us are slim to none."

Kimmie burrowed closer. "It landed on Dorothy's house." This was a heck of a time to find out how good a speller her child was.

Riley frowned. "Who's Dorothy? Someone in Charity City?"

"No, a character in *The Wizard of Oz,*" Abby clarified.

"Oh." He stood and looked down at Kimmie with what could only be described as a tender expression. "That's just a movie."

Kim met his gaze. "I know. But I've seen real lightning. And real thunder. Then the wind gets real bad. It knocked down my grandma's fence and blew her roof off. It's real scary."

He looked at Abby. "It did," she confirmed. "A couple years ago, there was a bad storm that spawned twisters in several areas around here. Kimmie was little, but she never forgot."

"Kimmie, it's a fact," he said, "that every year more people are killed by lightning than tornadoes."

"Mommy?" Her voice was just this side of full on hysteria. "I wanna go home."

"Good one, Ace." Abby glared at him.

"It's statistically true."

"And chronologically she's six."

"Mommy," she said, "I really, really wanna go home. I don't wanna stay out here. Please?"

Abby pulled her daughter into her lap. "Remember, Kim, you need to do a hike, then spend one night camping outdoors. We can't do it in our backyard because that's cheating. If we don't do this, you won't get your survival badge."

"I don't care," she wailed. "I wanna go home."

She looked at Riley. "What do you think?"

He glanced at the sky. "Right now, we have enough light to make it to camp and set up. Once we have shelter, we can wait it out," he suggested.

"If it doesn't blow over, she'll be hysterical all night. And the trauma of that could be worse than winding up in Oz."

Riley ran a hand through his hair. "It's your call. But you have to make it quick. If we wait too long, it'll be dark. And hiking back to the car under those conditions would be more dangerous than riding out the storm."

"Kimmie," Abby said. "You need to really think about this. If we don't stay, you're not going to get your badges."

After a rumble of thunder that sounded a little closer, Kimmie looked up, her lips trembling. "I wanna go home."

Abby held her close. "The thing is, she's been up since oh-dark-thirty. And she's not used to this much prolonged activity. She's not capable of a rational decision. But I won't force her to do this."

"Okay." He nodded. "Let's go back."

Abby took care of the blisters and they were out of there quickly. Adrenaline moved them along, and there was little dissension in the ranks. They made pretty good time back to the car, then headed for Charity City. It seemed a short time before Riley pulled up in front of the house. He carried their backpacks to the front porch and set them down. Abby unlocked the door and Kimmie raced inside.

"Thanks for trying," Abby said, looking up at him.

"I'm sorry." He didn't look sorry. He still looked tall. "For the record, I did take you. That fulfills my obligation."

"Yeah." She cocked her thumb over her shoulder. "I better make sure Kimmie's okay."

He nodded and jogged down the steps to his car. Biting her lip, Abby watched his taillights as he slowed for the Stop sign at the end of her street. It bothered her that he thought of them as an obligation. She didn't like being a burden to anyone. But she had her own burdens to worry about. How was she going to make sure Kimmie got her badge now? And how many cold showers would she have to take to freeze out memories of a man like Riley Dixon?

Chapter Three

Charity City High hadn't changed much since he'd been a student there. Riley was back, this time to work up a detailed security recommendation since he had a signed contract from the Board of Education. After they approved it, he'd install all the systems on campus. The library was his last stop and he scoped it out, vaguely remembering the last time he'd seen it. Scoping out had been his mission then, too—a girl, a cheerleader. He'd been pretending to study for finals.

Tall shelves of books still lined the perimeter of the room with more shelving taking up space in the center. Tables and chairs filled the rest of the area. One difference was the cubicles with computers against one wall. But the librarian's work station was still an oblong area just inside the door. That was going to have to be moved to make room for metal detectors.

It was about 4:45. The principal had told Riley that

class let out around three and by five the campus would be locking down for the night. The fewer students around for his evaluation, the better. Right now, the library was empty.

Maybe not so much, he thought as a familiar slender figure rounded one of the book shelves. Abby. The sight of her spiked his pulse as surely as shouts of incoming enemy fire. At the same time, he felt all the blood in his body head for points south of his belt. It had been a week since the aborted camping trip and just that morning he'd flattered himself that stray thoughts where she was concerned were nearly under control. One brief glimpse of her put the lie to that fantasy. Which begged the question: what the heck was she doing here?

She looked up from the book she was scanning and faltered momentarily before continuing to the librarian's area. "Riley. Hello," she said, moving into the center of the work station. "What are you doing here?"

"I was about to ask you the same thing."

"This is where I work. I'm the librarian."

And that was the first time he realized that during their long hike, he'd never once asked her what she did for a living. So much for the attention to detail he'd always prided himself on. Abby Walsh was beating his pride to a pulp.

"Why are you here?" she asked again.

"I'm working, too. My firm was contracted by the school district to install security systems and procedures." He was surprised she didn't know. That meant communication from administration to the rank and file was a weakness. He'd look into that. "You weren't informed I'd be here today?"

"Maybe. I haven't had a chance to read the daily announcements," she admitted. "It's Monday and I hit the floor running."

"Noted." But unacceptable. Communication was a key ingredient in security. And an area of concern for his report.

Right now, he needed to assimilate the fact that his job had just gotten a little harder, and more interesting. Because it was one of the larger buildings on campus, the library would require a lot more of his on-site time. He already knew the job would take several months to complete. Now he'd learned Abby worked here, which meant he would see her a lot. He couldn't get her out of his mind when he didn't see her. How would he handle it when he did?

"Speaking of running," she said, "it's time for me to go." After grabbing her purse from the bottom drawer of a file cabinet by her desk, she rounded the counter and headed for the door. "Bye."

When the door was closing behind her, he scratched his head. That went well. "Not."

And here was his problem. He was actually sorry to see her go. It was a gut-level reaction—the surge in blood pressure at the first glimpse of her and the fact that he'd instantly recognized her. Then the way his spirits took a dive at the sight of her leaving. Obviously these feelings weren't mutual. Could she have raced out of there any faster? Just as well. He was here to do his job in the place where she worked. Nothing more.

It took him only a few minutes to finish his preliminary analysis of the premises. After making some notes, he headed out to where he'd left his car in the faculty parking lot. As he walked toward his SUV, he noticed the car he'd seen in Abby's driveway. In fact, he saw her behind the wheel and heard the sound a car makes when you turn the key in the ignition and nothing happens.

He stopped and tapped on the driver's window. When it rolled down, he said, "Car trouble?"

She sighed. "I kept hoping it would turn over if I tried long enough."

"I think the battery might be dead. Mind if I take a look?"

"Be my guest."

After she released it, he lifted the hood and glanced at the engine. There were no obvious loose connections. Nothing that gave him a clue why it wouldn't start—or an easy fix.

"What's wrong?" she asked, when he went back to her window.

"I wish I knew."

She sighed. "I thought you survival types could make anything work with a little elbow grease and spit."

"Only if we know what to spit on," he admitted. "But I'd put my money on a dead battery."

She opened the door and he stepped back so she could get out. "I guess I'll have to go to the office and use the phone. My cell phone needs a charge. Apparently I've got battery problems all around."

"Use mine," he offered.

"I don't want to inconvenience a busy man like yourself."

"No problem. I'm finished for the day." He held out his phone.

"Thanks."

She dialed a number, then explained her situation to whoever picked up on the other end. It must have been about child care because she told whoever it was she was going to be a little late picking up Kimmie. After flipping the cell closed, she held it out.

"What about your car?" he asked. As he took the phone, he could almost see sparks where their fingers brushed. The way her gaze skittered away from his told him she'd felt it, too.

"I'll go to the administration office and see if anyone's still there to help me. Doggone it, I was planning to get a new car as soon as I saved the down payment. This thing's got to last just a little longer."

"I know a good mechanic," he offered. "And he's not too expensive."

"Translation—he won't take advantage of a woman who doesn't speak fluent automotive."

"Pretty much." He saw her hesitate. "I could give him a call and have him swing by. If necessary, he can tow it into the shop."

"I guess I don't have much choice. And that sounded terribly ungrateful." She sighed. "Thank you. I'd appreciate that."

"Okay." He flipped the phone open and checked his speed dial list until he found the number he wanted and pushed the connect button. Then he arranged to have her car looked at. "Bob will be here in about forty-five minutes to check it out. If it is the battery, he'll pop one in for you."

"Good. Thanks." Then she frowned. "But I can't wait for him. I have to pick up Kimmie before six. That's when her day care closes."

"You don't need to be here. He'll check it out and give you the good, bad and ugly."

"That only solves one of my problems. I have to get to Kimmie's day care."

"I'll take you." The words rolled out of his mouth before he could stop them. But he wouldn't have stopped them even if he could have. A guy didn't abandon a lady in distress.

She shook her head. "I've already inconvenienced you enough."

"No inconvenience. It's quitting time."

"Then you're probably anxious to get home. I'll just call a friend to get Kimmie."

"But I'm already here. Ready, willing and able. Why drag someone else out?"

"I don't know. It's just—"

"Look, you can beat around the bush for a while if you want. I can't stop you. But the bottom line is I don't mind and if you say the word, we can get your daughter before she's even aware there's a problem."

This was where he was getting into dangerous territory. It wasn't abandoning her if she had someone else to call. But he'd just made a case for her to accept his help. Above and beyond the call of duty. Damn it. Every time he did that, it bit him in the backside. And the high level of anticipation for her affirmative answer told him exactly how ready, willing and able he was. It also told him how much he needed to keep his mouth shut from now on.

He watched expressions come and go over Abby's face. And she had one very beautiful, very expressive face, he noted. He could see her reluctance to take anything from him, for which he couldn't blame her. His charm, and he'd been told he did have some, had been in short supply whenever he'd been around her. He saw apprehension in her eyes and wondered what she was afraid of. Finally, he noted capitulation when she realized he was right.

"If you're sure—" She chewed the corner of her lip as she met his gaze.

"If I wasn't, I wouldn't have offered. My car's over here."

She followed and he opened the passenger door of his SUV. She started to step up, then hesitated. Instantly he saw her dilemma. The tight skirt, while pleasing to his eye, would make it a challenge to get into the vehicle without compromising her modesty.

He put his hands at her waist and said, "Allow me."

Before she could protest, he lifted her onto the seat. She swung her legs inside, and he shut the door. He jogged around the car and got in. In spite of his warning, he felt oddly pleased about this turn of events. It was times like this when being a man of action was good. Act first, think later.

"Thanks for the lift," she quipped.

"You're welcome." He just hoped his impulsive good Samaritan routine didn't land him in do-gooder hell.

After Riley shut her door, Abby wanted to fan herself and chirp fiddle-de-dee. Was there anything that made a woman feel more womanly than a man who could practically span her waist with his hands, then actually lift her off her feet without grunting, groaning or asking what she'd been eating lately? Her heart hammered and she struggled to get it under control. She needed a distraction. Talking would be good. It would probably make the drive less awkward, too.

"Thanks again for the lift," she said, when he got in.

His responding grin liquefied her insides.

"No problem."

"Car trouble is part one of my worst nightmare."

He glanced at her, then returned his gaze to the road. "What's part two?"

"That I can't get to my child for some reason. Heart attack, car accident. Some trauma that keeps me from her and she's waiting all alone and scared because she doesn't know why I'm not there."

He smiled. "You're a little young for heart trouble."

Not so much, she thought, studying his oh-so-masculine profile. The rugged chin and well-shaped nose with a slight bump that told her it might have been broken. His five o'clock shadow that was right on time. The Sir Galahad routine. Under these circumstances, she could be just the right age for heart trouble. And he was just the guy who could give it to her if she wasn't careful.

"I worry." She shrugged. "Can't help it."

"You're a mom. No need to apologize. Your devotion to your daughter is commendable."

"Then why are you frowning?" she asked, studying the dark intensity on his face. "Were you raised by wolves?"

Briefly, he met her gaze, then shuttered the darkness that had glittered in his eyes for a split second. "Not wolves. I was adopted."

"Nora, too?"

He shook his head. "My parents thought they

couldn't have kids, so they adopted me. Then they got pregnant with my sister and life changed."

"Babies have a way of doing that." She noticed the muscle in his lean cheek contract and figured there were some memories he wasn't sharing. "To quote my daughter, you have to learn to live with disappointment."

"She was pretty clear that her father let her down." He met her gaze then, and one of his eyebrows lifted at what he saw. "Are you living with the same disappointment?"

"Not any more. I've put it behind me."

"That's not what the bite in your voice says."

"You're not going to drop this, are you?"

"It's not my plan," he agreed. "And we're ten minutes from day care so I have plenty of time to carry it out."

"Okay, then. Here's the scoop. But I need to warn you it's pretty pathetic." She sighed. "Fred Walsh was— probably still is—a good-looking, macho type. Like you," she added.

"You think I'm good-looking?"

She huffed out a breath. "Like you don't know."

He grinned again. "Thank you. But based on the mocking tone of your voice, I'm not sure I'll cop to it."

"You were an Army Ranger. If the combat boot fits—" She shrugged. "Anyway, Fred and I are complete opposites who somehow hooked up in high school. When I got pregnant with Kimmie, we got married."

"I see."

"The odds of success were not in our favor. To be fair, I give him points for duty and sticking with us until I finished college and started working at the high school."

"Then what?"

"He decided it was his turn. He wants to be an actor.

So he went to California for an audition for one of those survival-based reality shows. Figured he'd get noticed and a career would be born."

"And was it?"

"Not that I'm aware of. Although he found a woman to be his partner for couples stuff—you know, eating bugs and dropping out of the stratosphere from a dirigible."

"I can see you're not bitter."

"Does it show?" She smiled. "I did care and I can't help feeling betrayed. When he didn't come back, I got a divorce. That part was between adults, but there are no names bad enough to call him for what he did to his daughter. He signed away his parental rights because he didn't want to pay child support. I haven't talked to him in almost two years, and I'm okay with it. But he's turned his back on Kimmie."

He glanced at her, then pulled into the parking lot of Kimmie's day care. "Like I said—I'm glad you're not bitter."

Animosity welled up inside her. "He promised Kimmie he'd be back. I'll never forgive him for breaking his word to her."

"That stinks."

She reached for the door handle. "Yeah, it does."

"What did you tell her?"

"That her father loves her very much, but he has a dream and can't make it come true in Charity City."

"Does she buy into that?"

"You heard her. She remembers that her dad promised to come back and didn't. I won't bad-mouth him. But I can't give her what he won't. And—to quote you—it stinks." She glanced at him. "But Kim and I are fine. We don't need him or anyone else."

"If you say so."

"What does that mean?"

"I'm the guy you bought at the auction because you needed a wilderness guide."

"And look how well that turned out."

She opened the door and slid out. Unlike relationships, getting out of the car was a lot easier than getting in. Which was why she didn't plan to get sucked into another one—relationship, that is—especially with a man like her ex.

Riley pulled up in front of Abby's house and turned off the engine. He glanced to his right as she unfastened her seat belt. "So, Bob put in a new battery and the car's good to go. But it's at the high school. Are you sure I can't run you over there?"

She shook her head. "Your white hat is getting whiter by the second. But you've done more than a good guy's fair share. I'll have no problem getting a ride to school in the morning." She glanced over her shoulder at the child who'd been pretty quiet since getting in. "C'mon, Kim. I'll call Caitlyn's mom and see if we can hitch a ride to the The Bluebonnets meeting tonight."

"I don't want to go."

"Why not?" Abby asked. "You love the meetings."

"I don't feel good."

"Is it your tummy?"

"Kind of."

"You're probably just hungry. I'll make some soup and toasted cheese sandwiches."

"I don't want to eat."

"That's not what you said when I picked you up at day care. You told me you were starved."

"Not any more. Can I stay home tonight?"

"Let's eat and see how you feel."

"I'm not gonna feel any better. Why can't we just not go?"

Riley couldn't help overhearing the exchange since Kimmie wasn't moving at the speed of light to undo her seat belt. No one could accuse him of having the inside track about kids, but he had a feeling he knew what was bothering her.

"Caitlyn's getting her last badge tonight, isn't she, Kimmie?" he asked.

"Yup," she mumbled.

Abby's gaze snapped to his. "How did you know that?"

"You mentioned it. That night I stopped by the house."

The night he'd been sucked in by a little girl who'd seen more than she should of disappointment. Now she was facing more she'd have to live with. And he felt some responsibility. He wouldn't take responsibility for her blisters or for Mother Nature and the stray storm that had freaked the little girl out. But he could have done more to make it easier for her to be successful. This wasn't the time to figure out why he hadn't. He needed to make it right.

Abby opened the rear car door. "Kimmie, I thought you liked The Bluebonnets."

"I do, but…" She sighed. "It won't be the same if I'm not with Caitlyn."

"So you're giving up?"

"It's for the best."

Like mother, like daughter, he thought, wondering how many times the little girl had heard that phrase.

"But, Kimmie," Abby said, "I know how important this is to you. We can figure something out. Walshes don't give up."

"Daddy did. If he was here, probably it would be different. But we don't know how to be campers on our own."

That did it. Riley got out of the SUV and went around to the rear passenger door where Abby was standing. He looked at the little girl, into eyes so like her mother's and filled with the same shadows.

"Here's the deal," he said. "No one gives up. Not on my watch. You're going to get the badges you need."

"She is?" Abby looked surprised, with a little skepticism thrown in.

"I am?" Kimmie looked surprised, with a little hope around the edges.

"You are. We're going to hike to the campsite and spend the night outdoors so you can go on to the next level with your friend."

"But I got scared. We stink at camping," the little girl reminded him. "We were really bad at it."

"That's partly my fault," he admitted.

Because he wanted it over with, he'd thrown them into the deep end of the pool. Never test the depth of the water with both feet. He'd read that somewhere and thought it good advice. But it's exactly what he'd done with these two beginners. If he'd prepared them adequately, Kimmie wouldn't have been so frightened by the storm. Knowledge is power. "This time," he explained, "we're going to train before we go camping."

Kimmie's face brightened. "We are?"

"We are?" Abby echoed.

"Yeah. Like athletes do for a big race. Like they do for the Olympics. You can't just go out and win a medal. You need to get your body ready."

Standing this close to Abby, his was ready. But not for any athletic competition. Although what he was ready for could be defined as athletic. But that was something he would never let her know. He wouldn't let this get personal. This was about a little girl and her dreams. He'd screwed up. He would make it right.

"We're going to go camping. You're going to get your badges. And failure is not an option."

"Thank you." Kimmie hopped out of the car and hugged him. "Oh, boy!"

Yeah, oh, boy, he thought. Abby didn't have a monopoly on the hugging thing. And for the second time since meeting her, he hoped he didn't regret the decision he'd made.

Chapter Four

After sending Kimmie upstairs to change clothes and wash up for dinner, Abby turned on Riley. "Okay, what's all this about?"

He leaned back against the island in her kitchen and folded his arms over his chest. "Define 'this.'"

She didn't mean all the masculinity crammed into her kitchen that made concentration a challenge. That was for her to know and him to never find out. "This," she said, stretching out her arms to indicate the big picture. "Telling Kimmie she's getting her badge. No failure on your watch. What's up with that?"

"It's what I should have done in the first place."

"Which is?"

"When I donated the weekend to the auction, I figured some guy who liked camping would buy it. I'd sharpen his outdoor skills and give him a few pointers. We both know that's not what happened."

"Yeah. We both know a woman with absolutely no knowledge of outdoor activities bought the weekend for her equally fresh-air challenged daughter. And I say again, what's your point?"

"You needed the skills before deployment. The two of you are out of shape and that put you at a disadvantage from the get-go. I should have known better."

There was a lot of that going around, Abby thought. She should have known better than to count on anyone besides herself. Yet here she was listening to him and actually considering giving him another chance. And the child was right; they were bad at camping. If she was going to be successful, they needed Riley Dixon.

Abby hated that she couldn't be everything to her daughter. But because she couldn't, she was listening to this good-looking macho type. It had nothing to do with the fact that he made her heart flutter and her stomach lurch as if she were on the express elevator in a skyscraper. It was because she wanted her daughter to be happy.

But she was skeptical, too. His timing seemed a little suspect. The sad and pathetic details of her life with Fred The Flake had barely left her mouth when he decided failure wasn't an option. He had assumed some responsibility for their first failure, and she knew that was baloney. In order to get her badge, Kimmie only needed to hike three miles. For various reasons, none of which were Riley's fault, she'd been unable to accomplish that. He'd met his obligation, yet was now offering to give them more time than she'd paid for. She had to assume it was simply because he was a nice man. She desperately wanted back the stubborn slacker-jerk she'd first met. He was no threat to her emotional well-being. This man was a clear and present danger.

She moved around the island, putting as much tile-covered countertop as possible between them. "Okay, I need to know."

"What?"

"Do you feel sorry for me?"

"Why would you think that?"

"Come on. I'd barely finished telling you that my story was pathetic when you arbitrarily came to the conclusion that Kimmie needs to have her camping experience. And be successful," she added, remembering the outdoor fiasco. "So I need to know if you're doing this out of pity because it—"

He reached across the island and touched a finger to her lips, stopping the flow of words along with her heart. "I don't feel sorry for you," he said.

When he removed his finger, it took her a moment to catch her breath before going on. "It's okay for me to say my story is pathetic. But it's not okay for you to give us special treatment because of it. I can take care of my daughter by myself. There's more than one way to get from point A to point B. And sometimes it takes Plan B after Plan A doesn't work out." He stared at her for several moments after she finished. "What?"

"I was just waiting to see if you'd run out of steam."

She let out a long breath. "I'm done now."

"Okay." He leaned his forearms on the island. "This isn't about you. Or me. It's about that little girl. About learning she can do anything she sets her mind to. And about not giving up."

"I was right. It is pity," she said, shaking her head.

"It's about what's right. I messed up. I want to rectify the mistake."

Speaking of mistakes, the potential for a really big one was standing a foot and a half away from her. What he was proposing meant they'd be spending time together. Not thirty minutes ago, she'd told him he reminded her of her ex-husband. She often told her students that mistakes were how you learn, but making the same one twice was just dumb. Yet here she was, seriously considering letting him into her life to get her and Kim ready for a camping weekend. How dumb was that?

There had to be another way. "Riley, it's very noble of you to offer. But—"

"I'm hungry, Mom. When's dinner gonna be ready?" Kimmie climbed up onto a bar stool on the other side of the island next to Riley. This was a completely different child from the one who had had a tummy problem just a while ago.

How could Abby disappoint her when this man was offering to give up far more time than she'd paid for? He'd make her little girl's dream a reality. But would that give Kimmie the message that she needed a man to make all her dreams come true? Or was Abby overintellectualizing the situation?

"Mommy? Can Riley stay for dinner?" Kimmie turned puppy dog eyes on her.

Abby hated puppy dog eyes. "He might have other plans."

"Do you?" the little girl asked, looking up at him.

He shook his head. "I'm free for the evening."

"Mommy makes really good toasted cheese sandwiches. Sometimes she puts bacon on them. One time she put strings on—"

"Alfalfa sprouts," Abby clarified.

"Right. 'Falfa spouts," Kimmie said. "That wasn't so good. But mostly I really like 'em. Do you like toasted cheese sandwiches?"

"My favorite," he answered.

If she refused to feed him she'd look like the Wicked Witch of the West. Especially after he'd bailed her out with her car. Abby knew when she was between a rock and a hard place.

She looked at the tall, hunky, ex-military type and tried to put the right amount of welcome into her voice. Too little would sound ungrateful. Too much would tell him how much she hoped he'd say yes. Neither was an option.

"You're welcome to stay," she said.

"I'd like that a lot."

"Ya-ay." Kimmie clapped her hands.

"Then I can give you a ride to the meeting," he said.

Transportation was the least of her concerns when she had a man like Riley Dixon within spitting distance and staying for a meal. But apparently she'd need to learn to live with those concerns because he was going to be around a lot. There was no way she would turn him away and risk erasing the happy expression from Kimmie's face. No way.

"I'd appreciate that," she said. "And we can map out a plan of attack for our training."

"Plans are good," he agreed.

Yes, she thought. And her plan didn't include letting him too close to her heart. But maybe she was overreacting. He hadn't shown the slightest interest in her, at least nothing of a personal nature. One could only make a mistake if one had someone like him to make a mistake with.

So she had nothing to worry about.

Riley stacked the outdoor gear he'd brought in a corner of Abby's family room. "We'll deal with that later."

"Can't we play with it now?" Abby asked.

Riley studied her—the sparkling eyes and barely suppressed grin. He knew she was holding it back because her dimples were deeper than usual. She was messing with him. Oddly enough, he didn't mind.

"That's something Kimmie would ask," he said.

"Busted."

Her smile broke free and dazzled him, nearly dropping him to his knees. The sooner he got this mission under way, the sooner it would be over and he could draw a deep breath.

"Where's Kim?" he asked.

"Putting on her sneakers."

"Are they the ones she's going to wear on the campout?" He met her narrow-eyed gaze and added, "So we don't have a repeat blister incident, she needs to break in the same ones she's going to use. New shoes are a bad idea."

"They're new now, but won't be by the time we go camping."

"Good. We're going to the park two blocks over. It has a quarter-mile track. This is a step-by-step process and playing with the camping equipment is way down the list. The first priority is getting into shape for the hike. Today, I'm going to see how much work we have to do."

"A lot," she informed him.

You wouldn't know it to look at her. She was slender and curvy in all the right places. Her shape looked perfect to him.

"I'll evaluate your fitness level, and every week we'll escalate the training program accordingly. First we'll see how many times you can make it around the track. Then every day we'll add a little more distance."

"Every day?"

He nodded. "You have to get your muscles accustomed to the activity, then challenge your body some more."

"We're not talking about running marathons, are we?" she asked, resting her hands on the hips he'd just admired.

"No."

"Okay. Kimmie's been walking since she was ten months old and I've been doing it—longer. I think we can handle this on our own. We don't want to tie up too much of your time."

He folded his arms over his chest as he studied her face and the slight pucker in her forehead that said she was concerned. Did she want to get rid of him? His gut told him that was an affirmative. But he'd bet his Distinguished Service Cross it wasn't because she disliked him. Not the way she was acting a few minutes ago, teasing and smiling. She'd forgotten to be wary and was having fun.

Nope. She liked him, but she didn't like that she liked him. Because he was the good-looking macho type. He still couldn't decide whether or not to be flattered and decided not would be best. Ignoring the information would be even better. Forgetting altogether was an uphill battle.

Kimmie's running footsteps were loud on the stairs. "Riley!"

"Hey," he said, unable to keep from smiling at her bright face.

"I'm ready. This time, I have the right shoes."

"I see that," he said, studying her sturdy, white athletic shoes. No pink anywhere.

"I made a command decision about shorts," Abby said. "It's warm outside. We're willing to take a chance that any rogue bushes, brambles and shrubs won't do much damage to our legs here in civilization."

"You're mocking me."

"Just a little," she said. "It's pretty hard to resist."

No one would accuse him of being an expert on social behavior, but he was pretty sure you didn't tease someone you disliked. The thought pleased him. "You've passed inspection. Attire approved for the mission," he said, trying to keep it light.

Not easy when his throat closed and his voice turned gruff. Until Abby mentioned legs, he'd been able to direct his attention away from hers. Now that was all he could think about. She had great legs. The part not covered by material was tanned and shapely. He could just see the spot where her hip started to curve and the glimpse made him ache for more. She was right about it being warm, but in his case the heat was all about looking at her.

"Let's roll," he finally said.

"Okay. I've got the picnic basket packed as ordered."

She grabbed it from the island. "And permission to speak freely, sir."

He barely held back a grin. "And what if I say no?"

"I have to ask anyway."

"Permission granted."

"Why was I ordered not only to pack lunch, but to put it in this basket?"

"A good soldier never questions orders." She opened her mouth to protest, but he stopped her with a finger pressed to her soft lips. It was the second time he'd done that and he liked it even more. Ignoring the shaft of heat that shot through him, he continued, "I know you're not a soldier. But I'm still in the command position. It's not necessary for me to explain orders, but it is necessary for you to follow them. However, in this case I'll make an exception and explain. The basket is a visual aid to demonstrate bulk and why big cereal boxes are incompatible with backpacking and survival necessities."

"Understood, sir." She looked at her daughter. "Are you ready to go, kidlet?"

"Ready." She looked at Riley. "I'll carry the basket. I'll show you I can take my cereal."

"Your call," he told her.

They headed down the street with the little girl huffing, puffing and moving the basket from one hand to the other. He wanted to reach out and take it from her but figured that would defeat the purpose of the exercise.

Half a block from the house, Kimmie stopped and the stubborn expression on her face reminded him of her mother. The little girl set the basket down. "I can't carry this any more."

"I'll get it," Abby said, grabbing the handle.

Without the bulk, Kimmie hurried ahead. He and Abby followed more slowly, with her hefting the basket's bulk.

"You may or may not believe this, but it goes against the grain to let you lug that." His palms itched to take it from her. "My dad taught me guys should carry stuff for girls."

"Then why aren't you?" she said, obviously short of breath from the exertion.

"I'm making an example of you. It's a technique used in military training."

"Why did you decide to go into the service? Did you not want to go to college?"

"Actually I had a scholarship—athletic and academic—to Texas A&M."

"Then why didn't you go?"

He shoved his hands into his pockets and watched Kimmie jump onto the park track. "I got in trouble."

"What kind of trouble?" she asked, her voice laced with surprise.

"I beat up a guy."

"Why?"

He glanced at her. "I caught him with my sister, trying to push her into something she wasn't ready for. He was eighteen, and she was barely in her teens. He was my friend. I brought him over to the house."

"So you protected Nora?" When he nodded, she said, "Then I don't understand how that adds up to trouble."

"His folks were prominent in the community and they threatened legal action. After arbitration and negotiation, it seemed best for me to leave town and join the army."

"Oh, Riley, that seems so unfair," she said.

He shrugged. "It worked out for the best. I liked the military."

"But your education," she said, her expression showing her distress for him.

No, not him. An educator's concern for a student's lost opportunity. "I went to college in the army. There are programs. I got a master's in business."

"I'm glad. But it still seems unfair. Essentially, they punished you for doing the right thing."

It had been his first lesson in how going above and beyond the call of duty could blow up in your face. But once hadn't been enough. He'd gotten a refresher course with Barb.

They finally reached the park, and he stopped by the picnic benches under the trees. "Didn't your mother ever tell you life isn't always fair?"

"Yes." She set the picnic basket down, then flexed her fingers. "But—"

"We're going to walk around the track and work on endurance," he interrupted, not wanting to rehash the past.

"I better intercept Kimmie. If she gets to the swings, you can forget about doing laps."

After she caught up with her daughter, Riley picked a starting point and set a slow but steady pace. Kimmie made it halfway around the track before her attention wandered and she slowed to pick up rocks, leaves and twigs. On the second lap, she decided to walk backward, do cartwheels and skip.

When they started a third, she said, "I'm tired."

He decided to explain pacing herself another time. "If you push yourself a little bit farther now," he said, "next time you won't get tired as soon."

"Maybe we should take a rest," Abby suggested.

"If your survival depended on it, would you take a rest?"

"Under certain circumstances. Isn't it advantageous to preserve one's strength?" she asked.

"Sometimes. But here's the thing. There have been stories on the news lately about accidents in remote areas. Cars going off the road in desolate places. It can happen, and survival depends on skill and knowledge."

"I've heard." She looked at her daughter, who was dragging herself along as if she were on her last legs. "So you're saying The Bluebonnets is more than the social lark I thought when she joined?"

"I hadn't thought about it that way. But, yeah. Kimmie might have done it because of her friend. But now that she's involved, there are practical reasons for learning these skills. Knowledge builds self-confidence."

"You have enough to build a skyscraper with nothing but toothpicks and chewing gum," Abby said, shading her eyes with her hand as she looked up at him.

He couldn't help it. He laughed. Out loud. "Very funny."

Instead of agreeing, she looked startled. "Wow."

"What?"

"I'm not sure I've seen you do that before."

"What?" he asked again.

"Laugh." She studied him. "There have been a few smiles and a couple of grins, but no laughter. You should do it more often. Looks good on you."

Was laughter so rare for him? Maybe. Riley wasn't sure. But he realized that being around Abby made the impulse natural. She was quick-witted, funny and pretty as a picture with her pink cheeks and strands of brown silky hair fluttering around her face. And always those dimples lying in wait to ambush him.

"I'm too tired," Kimmie said, stopping in front of him.

Riley was grateful for the interruption. That particular train of thought was like walking through a minefield. "We just have a little bit more to go."

"I can't walk any more." The little girl bent at the waist and let her upper body go limp, then swung her arms from side to side.

He looked down at her. "What have we here? Rebellion in the ranks?"

"Sounds more like whining to me," Abby commented.

He glanced at her, then down at her daughter. "Listen up. There's no whining in basic training."

"But—"

He held up a finger, and the child huffed out a breath before turning away. "We're going to finish a mile."

She stomped ahead, proving she still had some juice left. When she got close to the starting point that marked a mile around the track, she started to run. One minute she was fine, the next she'd gone down in the dirt.

"Kimmie," Abby said, running toward the little girl.

Riley kicked it into high gear, too, and with his long stride, he reached the little girl just moments before her mother. "You okay, kiddo?" he asked.

She nodded even as she cradled her leg. "Mommy, I hurt myself."

"Yeah, sweetie, I see that."

He could see, too. It was a pretty good scrape. Blood started oozing, then mixed with dirt and pebbles. It must sting like a son of a gun. Surprisingly, the child, so dramatic about being tired just moments before, was doing her darnedest not to let go of the tears that were gathered in her eyes.

"I think basic training is over for today," he said.

"But I didn't go over the finish line," she pointed out, sniffling. "And I'm not cryin'."

Close, he thought. But there were no actual tears, and he knew it hurt.

He was proud of her. "How about we go back to the house and have a lesson in wound care. If The Bluebonnets don't have a first aid badge, they should. It's important to know how to properly take care of scrapes so they don't get infected. Nothing can derail a mission faster than infections."

"Riley's right, Kim. Taking care of your injury doesn't mean you're a quitter."

He lifted the child in his arms. "Definitely not."

One of the reasons he'd decided to complete the mission was because he didn't want this little girl to embrace her father's example of giving up and walking away. Watching her stoic effort to hold herself together showed him she was a miniature Abby—gutsy and strong. Like mother, like daughter.

He wasn't a quitter, but you couldn't quit what you never started. And that was his goal. To not start something he had no intention of finishing with Abby Walsh. He'd committed to this assignment and he would go the distance. But even he had to admit, in all his years as a soldier, he'd never undertaken a mission quite like Operation Backpack Barbie and her single mom.

If he was going to complete this one without an emotional ambush, he needed to focus on the finish line and keep his guard up.

Chapter Five

"Bring her in here," Abby said, leading the way to the family room. "Just put her on the sofa. I'll get stuff to clean and disinfect her knee."

"Can I have a Band-Aid?" Kimmie asked as Riley followed directions and gently set her down.

The words stopped Abby on her way out of the room and she smiled. Kimmie loved Band-Aids and frequently her request was vetoed when she wanted one for a boo-boo invisible to the naked eye. "Of course you can have a Band-Aid."

Riley met her gaze and, surprisingly, there was a twinkle in his eyes. Imagine that. "In the army," he said, "it's regulation to cover a wound to keep out dirt."

Smiling, Abby went into the downstairs bathroom where she kept the supplies, but she could hear muffled voices from the other room. Apparently his monosyllabic tendencies didn't extend to children. The man was a complete enigma. First, he categorically had refused to do what he had volunteered to do; then he had done a complete about-face and taken them camping. It wasn't his fault the trip had been a dismal failure. He was in the clear. But instead of retreating, he had had another change of heart and decided to put in more time than originally donated so Kimmie could earn her badges. Abby just didn't get him.

She hurried back to the family room. When Riley moved and gave her the space to do the honors, Kimmie pulled her knee back. "I want Riley to fix my boo-boo. I want him to show me how he did it in the army."

"You don't have to," Abby said to him.

"I don't mind." He rubbed his neck and met her gaze. "I'm lying. I do mind. Don't get me wrong. I've done my share of first aid, but usually the limb in question was a lot bigger and—"

"The patients were soldiers?"

"Well, yeah. But it has to be done and if she wants me to…"

"Please, Riley," Kimmie pleaded.

"Okay." He looked around. "It would help if we prop her leg over the sink. I want to pour the hydrogen peroxide over it, and you probably don't want that on the carpet."

"It wouldn't be my first choice," she agreed.

He scooped Kimmie up again, carried her into the kitchen and set her on the counter. Then he gently stretched out her leg, bracing the back of her knee on the separator between the two sinks.

He picked up the bottle of disinfectant and studied

the little girl whose dramatic facial expression suggested she was expecting amputation without anesthesia.

"Keep in mind," Abby told him, "that Kimmie has a flair for the dramatic."

After a moment of assessment, he unscrewed the bottle's top and said, "Why don't you pour it on, Kimmie? If it stings too much, you can stop."

Kimmie looked deep in thought, then nodded solemnly. Riley held out the large, economy-sized bottle and helped her hold it. If there was stinging, Abby couldn't tell. Her daughter concentrated on pouring the liquid, completely distracted from any discomfort. Stroke of genius letting her help. They watched the disinfectant bubble and make clean tracks through the dirt on her leg. He took the gauze Abby held out and gently washed up the area, then checked to make sure there weren't any pebbles left in the scrape.

"Here's the antibiotic ointment," she said, handing him the tube.

"I wanna do it."

Riley nodded and handed it to Kimmie. She centered her attention on dabbing the goo over the scrape like Picasso spreading paint on a masterpiece. And he let her take all the time she needed.

Finally the little girl held out the tube. "I'm done. Ready for my Band-Aid."

Abby held up several. "Ariel? Belle? Or Aurora?"

"Belle," Kimmie said, tapping her lip with her finger. "No. I mean Ariel."

"You name your Band-Aids?" Looking confused, Riley glanced from her to Kimmie.

Abby couldn't help laughing. This had to be so surreal for him. "These are cartoon characters—the princess collection."

"Ah," he said, nodding with comprehension. "I should have known. Very appropriate."

"Ariel, it is," she said to the child.

"If it falls off," Kimmie said, "then I'll use Belle."

Abby handed the oblong package to Riley and watched as he performed the final step of first aid with the same gentle care he'd used from the start. He had large hands, very competent. Who knew such a big man could be so tender? So gentle? Did he take as much care when he made love to a woman? Was he as tender when stroking her body after kissing her senseless?

Her pulse spiked and she shook her head to clear it of the sudden unwelcome erotic images. If he'd been the same jerk/flake/slacker she'd met in his office that first day, she could easily have resisted him. But he wasn't. There were layers to him she'd never suspected. Yes, he was a gung-ho, gorgeous guy, but he was also conscientious and, she suspected, soft-hearted. All of this added up to the fact that she was in a whole lot of trouble.

"You're very good with kids," Abby blurted out, adding to her trouble quotient.

"Do you have any kids?" Kimmie asked him.

"No." The single word was clipped, and his mouth hardened into a straight line.

Interesting reaction from Mr. Cool, Abby thought. There was something he wasn't saying. But she didn't feel it was right to pry. She already knew he wasn't married. That left separated, divorced or already involved with someone. But she could almost see the wheels in Kimmie's head turning. And her daughter hadn't yet developed the filter between her brain and her mouth that screened out inappropriate questions. Abby braced herself.

Kimmie stared up at him. "Do you have a girlfriend?"

"No." This time the corners of his mouth softened and just barely curved up.

Abby wanted to smile, too. Because he wasn't involved with anyone. It was stupid to be pleased that he was available, because he wasn't available to her. She wouldn't let him be. But, like her daughter, she was filter challenged. The one between her brain and her heart didn't do a great job screening out inappropriate attraction. She'd have to work harder at protecting herself.

Riley inspected Kimmie's knee. "I think you're going to live. But there might be a little scar."

Then he lifted her and started to set her on the kitchen floor. Kimmie wrapped her arms around his neck. "I don't know if I can walk."

"See?" Abby said. "A well-developed dramatic flair."

"I'll give you a ride to the sofa," he said, carrying her easily.

With her in his arms, he walked into the family room and settled her in a semi-reclining position on the sofa. At her direction, he slid a throw pillow under her knee. "She gives orders like a general," he commented.

"Tell me about it," Abby said.

He studied the little girl, then seemed satisfied that she was comfortable. Meeting Abby's gaze he said, "I guess I should go."

"No," Kimmie protested. "I don't want you to leave."

Neither did Abby. Although, unlike her child who put

into words whatever thought popped into her head, Chinese water torture couldn't drag the admission out of Abby.

"We're finished for today," he said, nodding toward her injured knee. "We should probably wait a few days to train again. When your knee doesn't hurt."

"But we haven't had lunch yet," the child protested. "Mommy made a picnic and we didn't eat it. There's a sandwich for you."

"Don't feel like you're on the spot," Abby told him. "However, I feel compelled to point out that she was a brave little soldier and such behavior should be rewarded. If you could possibly postpone whatever it is you have to do, there's a sandwich with your name on it."

He ran his fingers through his hair. "To be honest, there's nothing waiting for me but an empty apartment."

"Does that mean you can stay?" Kim asked.

"It does. And thanks," he said to Abby.

"My pleasure."

It scared Abby how very true those words were. She was way too pleased that he was sticking around, which meant she needed to get a handle on this—whatever it was—real soon. To do that she needed more information on him. More than the fact that he wasn't married and didn't have kids or a girlfriend. After making Kimmie comfortable on the couch with a movie in the DVD player, she went into the kitchen and Riley followed.

She unpacked the picnic basket and set out paper plates and napkins. "So you don't have a girlfriend," she said as casually as possible, continuing her six-year-old's interrogation. "Were you ever married?"

He stared thoughtfully at her. "I'm not exactly sure how that first statement leads into the question. But, yes."

So he was married once upon a time. "You're divorced?"

"Yes."

"And you never had children?"

"I believe that was asked and answered."

"So it was. It's just that you're so good with Kim. I can't help wondering how you got that way. Instinct? On-the-job training? Experience?"

He shrugged. "Maybe I'm a natural."

She tipped her head to the side and studied him. "You don't give out much information."

"Military training, I guess."

"So you can take the man out of the military, but you can't take the military out of the man?"

"So it seems." But his expression had turned dark, intense. Painful?

She didn't know him well enough to make a judgment about that. But she figured she'd inadvertently stepped into a verbal minefield. And it bothered her that she might have brought up memories that somehow hurt him. In spite of all her unanswered questions, she needed to put a lid on her curiosity and change the subject.

"I don't think I thanked you for carrying Kimmie home."

"My pleasure," he said, echoing her words.

"It wasn't a major trauma, and she could have made it under her own steam. But having your support made the whole situation less traumatic."

"Do you miss it, since the divorce? The support, I mean?"

Abby thought about the question. Her ex-husband had stuck with her until after she was settled in her job, but he'd never really been there. "You can't miss what you never had." She rested her back against the counter. "Fred was always off tilting at windmills and chasing dreams that never panned out. For all I know, he's still doing it."

She turned away so he wouldn't see anything in her eyes that she didn't want him to. Opening the cupboard, she reached for the tall iced tea glasses on the second shelf. They were just beyond her grasp and suddenly Riley was beside her.

"Let me," he said.

She stepped back, but not quite soon enough or far enough to avoid feeling the heat of his body. The way he filled out jeans and a T-shirt should be declared illegal. Before she could finish processing the thought and get over it, he pulled the glasses down and half turned so that their bodies brushed. Abby was sure that if it had been dark, she'd have seen sparks dancing between them.

Worse, the way his gaze narrowed told her he'd noticed the contact, too. His eyes locked onto her mouth and his chest rose and fell a little faster. He set the glasses on the counter and stared at her for a heartbeat. Then his head lowered toward her, just a fraction. She held her breath, wondering if he planned to touch his lips to hers.

"Mommy?"

The single word snapped him to attention. They jumped apart as if her father had suddenly appeared with a shotgun to defend her honor. Abby blew out a breath. "What, Kim?"

"I'm hungry."

"Lunch is ready."

As she hustled into the family room to take her daughter a plate, Abby wondered what had just happened. Had Riley been about to kiss her? She desperately wanted to believe the answer to that question was no because of how much she wanted it to be yes. She'd *wanted* to feel the touch of his lips to hers. Her profound disappointment at the interruption told her how wrong it would be to let this—whatever it was—between them get out of control.

Their relationship was task-based. When they'd reached their goal, all contact between them would cease and desist. She needed to remember that.

"Mommy says I can't play with matches," Kimmie said, brushing her brunette bangs out of her eyes.

Riley met her serious gaze. "These aren't matches. They're sticks. And if you rub them together hard and fast you get sparks. If the sparks are close enough to dry kindling, fire happens."

The little girl blinked up at him. "Mommy says you shouldn't play with fire."

The warning was too late, Riley thought, looking at Abby. He'd known she fell into the "playing with fire" category the moment he'd seen her. And nothing that had happened since had changed his mind. Especially the fact that the last time he'd seen her, he'd come close to kissing her. He hadn't planned to. But it set off a slew of warning bells that had reverberated through his system, followed by a solemn vow to never let it happen again.

"I already explained to Kimmie that fire isn't dangerous if you know what you're doing and you're careful. Want to help me out here?" he asked, unable to take his eyes off Abby's mouth.

"Nope. It's fun watching you try to reason with a six-year-old. Welcome to my world." Her wicked grin sent a shaft of heat straight through him. "Sorry. I couldn't resist."

That was tough for him, too. Especially when every time he glanced at her mouth, he wanted to take his solemn vow and shove it. But that thinking was counterproductive to today's operation. Kimmie's scraped knee had healed for several days and now he'd brought them back to the park for a lesson in the fine art and techniques of building a campfire.

Abby looked into the steel barbecue pit provided for public use by the park service. He'd assembled rocks and placed them in a circle with dry leaves and kindling in the center. The configuration was waiting for sparks, and there were plenty arcing between him and Abby.

She tipped her head a little as she studied him. "Tell me again why we need to know this. Why can't we just use matches?"

"What if you lose them or they get wet?"

"Let them dry?"

He shook his head. "They're no good."

"You'll be with us and you know how to start a fire with sticks," she argued.

"What would you do if something happened and I was incapacitated?"

"Does that mean you might get hurt?" Kimmie asked, looking worried.

"Sweetie," Abby said, pulling her daughter against her side, "Riley is just playing 'what if.'" She shot a glare in his direction. "Nothing's going to happen to him."

"So you can see into the future?" he asked.

"Of course not. But what are the odds? It's one night."

"Obviously The Bluebonnets believe the outdoor experience is important. Fire is necessary for warmth and cooking. It's a valuable skill to have."

Abby slipped her fingertips into the pockets of her short denim skirt. Her sleeveless pink T-shirt tucked into the waistband showed off her slender figure to perfection. Sneakers and socks completed the outfit courtesy of their daily walking routine. The fire lesson had only occurred to him the night before.

"I agree that it's important for kids to experience a lot of things," Abby said carefully. "And after this, Kim can decide if camping is a hobby she wants to pursue. But I'd be willing to bet that after she gets her outdoor badge, we won't be spending much time on the prairie."

He'd thought about that himself. "Still, you're talking about The Bluebonnets here. The outdoor badge is earned for surviving off the land. Fire is a part of that, and should be badge-worthy."

He was making a case that this was an essential lesson and he wasn't sure why. Did he need to justify spending time with Abby and Kimmie? They made him laugh and feel like part of a family. He'd forgotten how that felt. But could they have skipped this lesson on fire? Or was he complicating the need for this skill because a day without Abby was like a day without color and light?

"Let me get this straight," she said. "You're telling me... Fire good."

Her caveman voice left a lot to be desired, but it

made him laugh. "That's exactly what I'm saying. As well as, fire dangerous."

"Mommy, can I go play on the swings?"

Abby's gaze swung to the playground area, which was a few feet away. "Okay. Be careful."

"I will." She jumped into the large circle filled with sand and swings as well as a contraption for kids to climb on.

"I can see she was completely riveted by the presentation," he said wryly.

"Short attention span. Don't take it personally."

None of this was personal, but the challenge was remembering that. It was all about duty, honor and the Charity City auction, he reminded himself. Then he watched Abby watch her child play. He noticed the tender, loving expression on her face, the way her dimples deepened and her mouth curved up in a small smile. Her full lips were the stuff of male fantasy, so full and soft-looking.

And suddenly it all felt very personal.

So he reminded himself again that he was only a volunteer here because the foundation that dispersed auction proceeds had given him start-up capital for his business. Which reminded him of something else.

He folded his arms over his chest and leaned against the end of the picnic table, crossing one ankle over the other. "The Charity City Chamber of Commerce is having a dinner meeting on Saturday night."

"That's nice," she said, distracted as she waved at Kimmie.

"It's a welcome for Dixon Security, along with an invitation to become a member of the chamber."

"Good for you." She nodded and smiled when Kimmie shouted to look at her.

"Yeah. It's important for a businessman to be involved with organizations like that. The networking is critical for growing the business."

"I can imagine."

"So would you like to go?"

Her gaze snapped to his. "What?"

"The dinner. Saturday. Would you go with me?"

"I'm a teacher—specifically, a librarian. I don't know anything about business."

He ran his fingers through his hair. "Business aptitude isn't a prerequisite for eating. Actually, the constitution of an elephant would be more helpful than business sense. To digest the rubber chicken and cold potatoes," he explained, feeling pretty lame.

He was sorry he'd opened his mouth, but it was too late now.

She frowned. "I don't understand."

"It was English, not Swahili," he said, annoyance at himself kicking up even more. "I asked if you'd accompany me to a town function. There's not much to understand."

"But that's not part of the responsibility I bought."

"Understood." He met her gaze. "So what about the COC dinner?"

She absently tucked a strand of hair behind her ear. "Did we or did we not agree that our relationship is task-based. We've come together to make sure Kimmie gets her outdoor experience?"

"We did." He couldn't be sorrier that he'd started this. "Look, Abby, a simple yes or no will suffice."

"Okay. No."

He felt as if she'd slugged him in the gut. "Okay. Well…" If he had a foxhole handy, he'd dive in head-first and wait for the concussion from the explosion.

Then Abby started laughing. "How does it feel, big guy?"

It feels pretty damn bad, he wanted to say. Rejection is lousy. But instead, he said, "How does what feel?"

"When you're told no. The shoe is on the other foot. How do you like it?"

"So this was an object lesson based on my behavior from our first meeting? Behavior for which, correct me if I'm wrong, I've already apologized?" The knot in his gut loosened.

"Pretty much. It's what I do with Kimmie. Sort of a how-would-you-feel-if-someone-did-that-to-you thing."

"I see. So, now that you've had your object lesson, what do you say to a really bad dinner and boring speeches on Saturday night?"

"I say—okay."

"Good," he said, hoping he didn't sound as glad as he felt.

"But only to quiet the rampant rumors that you're gay."

He stared at her and must have looked horrified, because she started laughing again. He knew she was teasing, but a rumor like that couldn't be more wrong. If he'd kissed her the other day, his sexuality wouldn't be in question. He'd never wanted anyone the way he wanted Abby. His gut-level disappointment at her teasing turndown proved it.

But now he'd opened his big mouth and she'd agreed to go. So he needed to go to Plan B—no extracurricular survival training. Get Kimmie her badge and walk away. Like a good soldier. No more playing with fire.

He just hoped he could get through dinner Saturday night without getting burned.

Chapter Six

Abby had a glass of wine in one hand and her tiny black satin evening clutch in the other. In the banquet room of The Homestead, the Charity City restaurant where the Chamber of Commerce held its monthly meeting, she stood quietly off to the side. The place was rustic yet charming, with a ceiling two stories high comprised of rough-hewn beams and walls covered in elegant, flowered wallpaper.

Her comfort zone was near the huge fireplace where a cheerful fire crackled. The warmth felt good since a cold front had come through that day, lowering the daytime temperature. Round tables covered in white linen were arranged in the center of the room and set for the upcoming dinner. And vases with fresh flowers were scattered everywhere, filling the air with a fragrant scent.

Roy and Louise Gibson, owners of the restaurant and parents of her good friend, were bustling around the room making sure no one needed anything. It might be a business dinner, but they were determined to make it personal. And speaking of that, Riley had been involved in conversation with a group of men on the other side of the room practically since they'd arrived. She couldn't decide whether to be annoyed or relieved.

When the Gibsons stopped beside her, she was thankful she didn't have to choose. Louise was small and round, with short thick, brown hair shot with red highlights. Roy was two or three inches taller than his wife, and also round. He was balding, and what hair he had was silver. Their gift of making business personal had rubbed off on their daughter, and Jamie's folks were two of her favorite people in the world.

After exchanging hugs, Louise said, "I haven't seen you since the night of the auction. What have you been up to?"

Abby remembered that night. Her glance strayed to Riley's broad back and a ripple of excitement shivered through her, reminding her of the thrills and chills the mayor had promised on Riley's behalf. She hadn't spent an entire weekend with him, but she'd certainly had her share of chills. But that reminded her. She was curious about why Roy and Louise had persevered against all comers at the auction to walk away with an ex-cop.

"I've been busy with school and Kimmie," she answered vaguely. "Now that you mention it, I've been meaning to ask if Jamie is happy with the cop you bought at the auction."

"I don't care if she is." The twinkle in Roy's blue eyes disappeared. "Her mother and I were worried. Weird things have been happening here at the restaurant and to Jamie."

"Define weird," Abby said, concern sliding through her.

"The restaurant was broken into."

"Was anything taken?" Abby asked, startled. She hadn't heard about it.

"A photo of Jamie from my desk," Roy answered.

"That's all?"

Louise nodded. "And we've had hang-ups. You know, where you pick up the phone and know someone's there, but they don't say anything."

A chill that had nothing to do with Riley slid down Abby's spine. "The last time I saw her, Jamie looked like there was something bothering her, but she wouldn't talk about it."

"That's our girl," Louise said, the ghost of a smile curving her mouth. Then it was gone. "She's too darn stubborn and independent for her own good. But we think she needs protection. She won't ask for help and doesn't want to bother us or cause us worry."

"So we took matters into our own hands," Roy explained. "Now she has a bodyguard."

"Wow," Abby said. Although she already knew, she asked, "How did that go over?"

"Like a fly in your consommé," Roy confirmed. "But that's too darn bad. She's our little girl. Whether she likes it or not, she's stuck with Sam Brimstone. If he can't get to the bottom of what's going on, we'll figure something else out. One way or another, we're going to make sure nothing happens to her."

"Good." Abby sipped her wine. "I'm concerned about her, too. I thought she looked too thin. Not good advertising for you two restaurant owners, I can tell you."

"Don't we know it," Louise agreed. "I feel better knowing Sam is watching over her. But what about you, young lady? What's with the hunk you bought at the auction?"

"Which hunk would that be, honey?" Roy asked, the sparkle back in his eyes. "She bought two. Remember?"

Apparently it was too much to hope no one remembered, Abby thought, cringing. "Only one was for me," she explained.

"Who's the other for?" Louise asked, a cagey look in her dark eyes.

"I'm sworn to secrecy."

"We already know you bought Des O'Donnell for Molly Preston. Don't look so surprised. We were there, remember?" Louise patted her arm. "Not to worry. We'll never tell. Des is certainly a good-looking young man."

Abby followed the other woman's gaze to the center of the crowded room where Riley was talking to Des O'Donnell, who'd recently assumed control of the family construction company after his father's death. "I have no idea why Molly wants to keep him under wraps."

"I'm disappointed in you, Abby. You're divorced, not dead," Louise said. "Use your imagination, dear."

"Mrs. Gibson!" Abby stared at her, surprised.

The older woman looked unrepentant. "What? I'm old, not blind. The one you bought isn't bad, either. What are you doing with him?"

"I don't have him under wraps." Not for lack of imagination, she thought. "He's helping Kimmie get her hiking and survival badges for the scouting group she belongs to," Abby explained.

"So you bought him for Kimmie?" Roy asked.

"That's right."

"Then how come you're his date tonight?" Louise raised one eyebrow.

Date? Why did there have to be a label? Why couldn't they just be two friends attending a dinner together? Her gaze swung back to Riley, standing slightly taller than the other men in the group. He wore a navy, double-breasted suit and red tie. His dark hair was neatly combed and he had a beer in his hand while he listened to something Jack Wentworth was saying.

Her heart stuttered, a sensation that was becoming all too familiar at the sight of Riley Dixon. But tonight it was even more so. He cleaned up good, really good, darn her luck. His familiar, rugged look—the only way she'd seen him until now—was enough to give females the world over heart palpitations. But this classy side of him was disconcerting, to say the least.

As the three men stood there, a flash went off, and Jack took the brunt of it. He grimaced and automatically raised his hand to block out the light. Although, of course, it was too late.

"That Mackenzie Andrews," Louise tsked. "She's been doing that to Black Jack Wentworth all night. If you ask me, she's using her position as society reporter for the *Charity City Chatter* to take shots at Jack. No pun intended. I think she's got something against him. He'll be lucky if he can see straight when she's finished with him."

"There's some history between those two," Roy agreed. "You know anything about it, Abby?"

"Hmm?" She'd been too focused on Riley to pay close attention to the conversation around her. "Not really."

"You gonna stare at him all night?" Louise asked.

"Who?" Abby blinked at the older woman. "Oh. Riley. You wanted to know why I'm here with him tonight," she reminded them, amazed that she remembered the question. "I'm here because he asked."

As if his ears were burning, Riley glanced in her direction and smiled. It threw Abby off-kilter, as if Mackenzie Andrews had just set off a flash in *her* face. Or maybe the wine had given her a lovely buzz, but she wouldn't bet on it. When Riley said something to the other men and walked in her direction, she braced herself.

"Hi," he said, stopping beside her.

"Hi. Do you know Roy and Louise Gibson? They own this restaurant," she said, indicating the older couple and the room around them.

"Riley Dixon." He shook hands with them. "Nice to meet you."

"Likewise," Roy said. "Welcome to the Charity City Chamber of Commerce. I understand you're real busy with that security business of yours."

"Yes, sir. Right now, I'm working on a system for all the high schools in the district."

"I heard. Walt Emerson is president of the school board. He comes in to eat a lot. Says they were impressed with the plan and procedures you presented."

"That's good to hear." Riley smiled at the other man.

"You know, son, some time soon I'd like to talk to you about updating the security system here in the restaurant."

"Be happy to discuss it with you, sir."

"It'll have to wait," Louise said, pointing. "Ella's trying to get our attention." She took her husband's hand.

"She's our hostess. And ten to one, there's a problem we need to deal with."

"Go," Abby said. "Don't worry about us."

"Nice to meet you, Riley," Roy said as his wife dragged him off.

"Same here, sir," he said, then met Abby's gaze. "Sorry I abandoned you."

"You didn't. It's called networking. And you were doing a fine job of it."

"That I was."

She drank the last of the wine in her glass. "How's it going?"

"Really good."

Just then, a flash went off in front of them, blinding Abby. When her vision cleared, she recognized Mackenzie Andrews.

"Sorry about the flash." The pretty brunette nodded with satisfaction. "But in underlit rooms like this, it's the only way to get a decent shot."

"Then you must have a whole bunch of decent shots of Jack Wentworth," Riley said.

The woman's gaze strayed to the tall, exceptionally good-looking son of the mayor. Her lip curled distastefully. "I certainly do."

"Mac, what have you got against Jack?" Abby asked.

"Long story. And I'm working." She shrugged and moved away to snap more pictures and take notes for her article.

"Hi, you two." Des O'Donnell appeared on the other side of her.

Abby hadn't actually met him. She recognized him from his photograph posted on the auction Web site.

She'd come across it when she'd been looking to buy a guy for her nature guide. Des's dark blond hair, blue eyes and cocky smile were even better in person. He was a pretty attractive man, and she figured Molly had noticed. Although they'd only become close friends in the last couple of years, Abby knew Molly pretty well. She didn't think her friend wanted Des for "under wraps," horizontal hula activities. But she had no clue what Molly planned to do with him. She only knew his company had been awarded the contract for the new wing of the pre-school where Molly worked.

"Hi, Des. Abby Walsh," she said, holding out her hand.

"Nice to meet you, Abby." He shook her hand and nodded to Riley. "I thought I'd never get away from that guy who's looking to build a room addition for a dollar and a half."

"How do you two know each other?" Abby asked, looking from one to the other. How often did a girl find herself sandwiched between two such good-looking guys? She barely resisted the urge to fan herself and sigh like a Southern belle.

Des grinned. "High school football. Riley was the team captain. I was the unfortunate underclassman he used for a tackling dummy."

"A gifted one as I recall," Riley said, grinning too.

"Yeah." Des glanced apologetically at her. "Sorry to talk more business, but I need Riley's help with some security concerns. O'Donnell Construction has equipment and supplies that are vulnerable to theft and vandalism during ongoing construction."

"Happy to help," Riley said.

"Sorry, Abby," Des said again.

"No, problem." She shrugged. "After all, this isn't social. It's business."

As a waiter walked by, Riley absently took her empty glass. He set it on the tray, then took another and handed it to her while listening to Des.

She was struck again by his intense good looks. But he was so much more than just another pretty face, she realized. Tonight she'd seen him mingle with the town's top businessmen and handle himself in a smart, professional manner. It suddenly hit her that she'd been unfair to put him in the same league as her ex-husband. The only things the two had in common were the buffness factor, a fondness for outdoor activities and exceptional good looks that tempted her and tested her mettle.

Now, talking to Des, she remembered what the mayor had said the night of the auction. Riley was a hometown boy. He'd left for the army, but he'd come back. And started a successful business. Unlike her ex, he wasn't a quitter.

He was nothing like Fred The Flake, and the realization knocked the props out from under her. She'd been hiding behind all her reasons for disliking him, and now she realized he wasn't what she'd thought at all. The information didn't make her a happy camper.

Hours later, when he pulled up in front of her house to drop her off, she was even less happy. Louise Gibson had called it a "date." At the end of an evening, usually one kissed one's date good-night. And sometimes one invited one's date in for a nightcap and other stuff. Kimmie was spending the night at her grandparents' house and Abby couldn't resurrect any of her former reasons for keeping Riley at arm's length. She didn't think she could survive another is-he-going-to-kiss-me moment. With nowhere left to hide, her only option was retreat and run.

As the car came to a stop, she opened the door. "Thanks, Riley."

"Wait," he said, turning off the ignition. "Let me walk you to the door."

She slid out of the vehicle onto the sidewalk and turned to look at him. "Don't bother. It's late and—"

"It's nine-thirty," he said wryly.

"Really? Wow. It feels late." She was grateful for the dark that kept him from seeing the flush creeping up her neck. "Thanks for a lovely evening."

She slammed the door and didn't hear his response. After hurrying up the sidewalk, she inserted her key into the lock. It took several tries before she was finally successful. Trembling hands had a way of slowing down even the most mundane task. Just before she walked inside, she glanced back and noticed he was still parked. When she closed the front door behind her, she heard his car pull away.

"Darn it. He's a gentleman to the last. That is so annoying."

Because it made keeping him at arm's length more challenging than ever. And what he must think of her, running inside like a scared rabbit. There's no way he wouldn't have noticed. But she couldn't afford to care what he thought of her. Better to look foolish than find out he kissed even better than she suspected.

Several days following the COC dinner, Riley rang Abby's doorbell and waited. When no one answered after a reasonable length of time, he glanced at her driveway even though he'd just passed her car. There was no doubt she was home. He'd called a little while ago to let her know he was stopping by to show them how to use the equipment he'd left a few weeks before. But with her skittishness when he'd dropped her off the other night, he could make a case for his warning making her beat a hasty retreat now.

He knocked again, then put his hand on the knob and turned, surprised when the door opened. "Someone else needs a refresher course on stranger danger," he muttered.

He walked through the house, not flinching this time at all the pink. It was sort of growing on him. "Hello?"

No one answered, but he heard laughter coming from the backyard and headed that way. Looking through the kitchen slider, he recognized his own ultralight two-person tent standing in the middle of the yard. Abby had unrolled one of the sleeping bags and was trying to fold it up again like a bath towel. Her struggle had Kimmie rolling on the grass, giggling.

"That's what happens when you jump the gun," he said, walking outside onto the patio.

Kimmie sat up. "Riley!"

Her face lit up at the sight of him, and he felt a tugging in the region of his heart. "Hey, kiddo."

"I thought you'd never get here." She jumped up and ran to him.

He picked her up, always surprised at how light she was. But there was nothing light about the feeling tightening in his chest when she put her arms around his neck.

"Me and Mommy need help."

He shifted her weight to his forearm so he could see

Abby on her knees in the grass. "You looked like *you* were having a great time," he said to the child. "But Mommy isn't having much fun, is she?"

"What was your first clue, hotshot," she said, huffing her bangs out of her eyes.

"I'm brighter than the average bear. Nice job on the tent. I'm impressed," he said, nodding in the direction of the nylon dome.

"The directions were clear and easy to follow." She glared at the sleeping bag. "Unlike this invention of the devil."

He set the little girl down and walked over to her mother. "It's a three-season bag with Polarguard Delta insulation that keeps you warm down to twenty degrees Fahrenheit. It has men's and women's designs."

She gave him a wry look. "Don't tell me. This is the men's."

"Right in one. How'd you know?"

"Because it's giving me problems and has the potential to become a major headache."

He laughed. "It also comes in regular and long lengths."

"This must be long."

"Right again. And what was your first clue?"

"Other than a visual," she said, "it won't fold up."

"So it's all the bag's fault?"

"Of course."

"Riley," Kimmie said, pulling on his hand, "can you fix it?"

"It's not broken." He smiled down at her. "But I can fold it up."

There was an expression on Kimmie's flushed face of utter and complete trust in him. The knot in his chest tightened again and turned painful. He thought about another child, one he'd loved and lost. The boy had been two when his biological father decided he wanted him. He would be about a year younger than Kimmie was now—talking coherently, having impressions of the world, starting school. Watching Kimmie reminded Riley how much he'd missed out on when he'd lost everything.

"So fold it up already," Abby said, tearing him from the painful thoughts of the past.

He sighed and squatted down, pressing one knee into the grass beside her. "Technically it's called compressing."

He started with the small end and rolled until it was a neat size that fit back in its carrying bag. "See?"

He looked into Abby's sparkling brown eyes and could see clearly for the first time in a long time. He could see how her father's indifference had hurt Kimmie. Maybe it was better for the boy he'd thought of as his own to have his biological father and not have to wonder where he was and why he didn't care.

Riley didn't need to see Abby's sweet, floral scent. The perfume distracted him from his emotional thoughts as it swirled in the air around him and made his skin tingle. Her dimples deepened when she smiled at him as if he'd done the most remarkable thing. Her full lips tempted him to taste what he'd been denied the other night when he'd dropped her off.

Until this moment, he hadn't realized how much of his day had been spent in a heightened state of anticipation. Not only that, he knew without a doubt if it hadn't been the camping equipment, he'd have found another excuse to stop by. And he was glad she hadn't come up with an excuse to avoid him.

The child he'd lost was in the past. Abby was now, and she was dangerous. Along with her pint-size secret weapon named Kimmie. Because he didn't want to care that much again. He didn't want anyone to become his whole world. When the campout was complete, he'd have no reason to see them again. The thought produced a hollow feeling inside him, proving now was the point of no return. He needed to shore up his defenses and protect his emotional perimeter before it was overrun by the dynamic duo.

"Compressing is impressive," Abby said. "You made it look easy. Why couldn't I do that?"

"I've had more practice. It's all in the wrist." He shrugged. "My hands are bigger, stronger."

"I'm getting stronger," Kimmie said. "Mommy and me walked around the track eight times and I didn't even get tired."

"Good for you," he said, watching her beam with pride at the praise.

"You know what would help you get even stronger?" Abby said. "A good night's sleep."

"Do I hafta?"

"It's time for your bath."

"But, Mo-om, Riley just got here."

He held up his hand. "A soldier never questions a direct order."

The little girl heaved a huge sigh, but didn't protest further. Although her body language spoke volumes. She turned and dragged her feet into the house.

"I'll be up in a minute," Abby called after her. She looked at him. "Again I'm impressed. What are you doing tomorrow night at bedtime?" Her eyes widened when the words sank in. "I mean Kimmie's bedtime—To get her to cooperate—Because sometimes there's rebellion in the ranks."

"I know." She hadn't meant anything personal, but parts of him wished very much that she had. She'd made it painfully clear the other night that she wanted nothing like that from him. So, he figured he'd gotten all the mileage possible out of his pitiful excuse for stopping by. Now it was time to evac.

"I'll help you bring all this stuff back inside before I go," he said to smooth over the awkward moment.

He took the tent apart and stowed it, then grabbed the sleeping bags. After neatly restacking the equipment in the living room, he ran his fingers through his hair. "I guess I'll go now."

She nodded. "I have to get Kimmie settled."

"Yeah." He glanced around the room. "So you guys did eight laps at the park?"

"Yes," she said proudly. "We walk every night after dinner."

"Good. Hiking is a little different, but you're building endurance and that will make it easier." He was stalling. It wasn't his finest hour.

She opened the door, but when he looked down at her, he noticed the pulse at the base of her neck was fluttering wildly. There was a lot of that going around. It was contagious and he'd definitely caught it from her.

"Okay, then. Pretty soon you two will be ready for take two on survival weekend," he said.

"Good." She looked up at him and it was all he could do not to pull her into his arms right then. "Thanks for everything, Riley."

"No problem."

He stepped out onto the porch and moved down the walkway. When he rounded his SUV, he looked back and saw her leaning a hip against the door. She looked all barefoot and sexy in those shorts that showed off her feminine curves just the way he liked them. The last time he'd been here, she'd hopped out and run inside as if the hounds of hell were after her. And he knew why. To avoid the awkward do-we-kiss-or-not moment at the front door. Ever since, he'd wondered what she would taste like and how she would feel with those curves pressed against him. The wondering had made for some long, painful and sleepless nights. Speaking of take two—he was back and no time like the present to take advantage of second chances. Then he could put the thoughts out of his mind.

So he jogged back up the walkway and stopped in front of her.

"Did you forget something?" she asked, surprised.

"Yeah." He put his hands on her waist and pulled her to him. "This."

He lowered his head and touched his lips to hers, tasting surprise followed by hesitation, then surrender. Her hands slid up his chest, around his neck, and he tightened his arms until daylight couldn't find a space between their bodies. She felt better than he'd imagined, her lips softer than he'd thought possible. Her rounded breasts burned against his chest, made his heart pound and put a hitch in his breathing.

Then he tangled his fingers into her hair, cupping the back of her head to make the contact of their mouths firmer. She moaned and brushed her palm over his neck, raising sparks that threatened to make him go up in flames.

"Mommy? I can't turn on the water."

The child's voice drifted down the stairs and pulled them apart. He knew an instant of satisfaction when he noticed that Abby's breathing was as ragged as his own. Not only that, her hand shook as she brushed the hair off her forehead.

She looked up at him, her lips parted and moist from his own. "I—I have to—" She waved her hand in the general direction of the stairs.

"Yeah. You have to—" He drew in a deep breath, struggling to fill his lungs with air.

"Bye, Riley." She shut the door.

Damn. If only she'd done that two minutes ago—before he'd seen her waiting and changed his mind about leaving. Now he knew what kissing her was like. Instead of putting an end to the wanting, all he could think about was doing it again—and again. It had been a big mistake, and he wished his resistance techniques had been stronger. Or that he could rewind and take it back.

Then he wouldn't have known this special kind of heaven mixed with a generous helping of hell.

Chapter Seven

"Hi, Abby."

Abby looked up from the computer at her desk in the school library to see Nora Dixon standing at the counter. It had been a couple of weeks since Dixon Security had started work at the school and this was the first time she'd seen Riley's sister here.

"Hi." She smiled, genuinely pleased. "It's nice to see you. What brings you here? I'm assuming it's not because you didn't have enough of high school the first time around."

Nora laughed. "No. One time through was plenty. Have you seen Riley?"

That was a loaded question. Abby hadn't actually seen him today, although she knew he'd been around campus working because she had the all-over tingles to prove it. Her Riley radar was on high frequency. So she hadn't laid eyes on him, but his image popped into her head constantly, followed by memories of *that* kiss. He was a good kisser, even better than she'd suspected—a fact that had disrupted her peace of mind more than once in the past week.

She stood and cleared her throat, composing herself as she walked closer to the counter. "I haven't seen him. Why don't you try his cell phone?"

"Yeah." The redhead set her purse on the counter separating the work area from the expanse of tables and rows of bookshelves. "I'll do that. How are you?"

"Fine. And you?"

"Riley said you went to the Chamber of Commerce dinner with him," his sister continued, ignoring the question. "Was it pretty boring?"

"What did *he* say?" Abby hedged, on her guard because the other woman seemed tense.

Nora shrugged. "He doesn't volunteer much information."

That was certainly true, Abby noted. She'd been on the receiving end of his noncommunication skills. What was the harm in telling his sister the truth?

"The speeches could have put an insomniac on caffeine to sleep," she said, pleased when Nora laughed and relaxed a little.

But Abby remembered that sitting beside Riley had been like a shot of adrenaline to her susceptible system and sleeping had been the last thing on her mind that night. The masculine scent of him, the heat of his body invading her own, the way he filled out his suit. That hadn't been the least bit boring.

"Why do you want to know?" Abby asked.

"He seems different."

"From what?"

"From the way he was." Nora's green eyes narrowed. "He seems happy lately."

"Well that explains it."

"What?"

"Why you look like you'd enjoy seeing me drawn and quartered in the town square at sunrise."

"Sorry." Nora had the grace to look sheepish. "It's just that it's nice to see Riley in a good mood. And I can't help thinking his recent state of mind has something to do with you."

In spite of herself, a glow started in the pit of Abby's stomach and the warmth spread through her. Riley was happy because of her? Why would that upset Nora?

"Well, I'm not sure how to respond to that. He's training Kimmie and I for the survival weekend I bought at the auction. But I'm sure you already know that. When he's finished, my daughter will get her scouting badge."

"And what badge are *you* after?"

Abby blinked. "Excuse me?"

"It wouldn't be the one that says Mrs. Riley Dixon, would it?"

Abby planted a fist on one hip as anger coursed through her. "I'm not sure that's any of your business."

"So I'm right."

"No, you're dead wrong. But it still doesn't concern you."

"That's where *you're* dead wrong. What other reason could you have for going to the Chamber of Commerce dinner with him?"

"Maybe because he asked me?" What was it with everyone in this town. First Louise Gibson. Now Nora.

"Well there's no maybe about this. He's my brother and I care about him."

Abby could respect that, but what did that have to do with her? Then she suddenly got it. "You didn't come here to see him at all, did you?"

"I came to warn you," Nora said.

"About what?"

"He's not as tough as he looks."

Abby shivered as an image of his muscular legs, wide chest and impressive biceps flashed through her mind. Wimps didn't make the cut to Army Ranger. Physically he was tough as nails. But she knew Nora meant relationship-tough. And that piqued her curiosity.

"There's nothing personal going on between Riley and me." Not entirely the truth, she thought, remembering the kiss. By definition, a pressing together of lips was personal. And when the person attached to those lips was Riley, it had felt pretty darn personal, too.

"You're a single mother, and single mothers tend to want the white picket fence and a father who goes to work to pay for it. If your feelings for my brother aren't sincere, back off. He was hurt before and I don't want to see it happen again."

Abby blinked. "What are you talking about?"

Just then, the brother in question came into the library, whistling a happy tune. He stopped short when he saw his sister. "Nora. What are you doing here?"

"I stopped by to see if I can buy you dinner," she said. Riley set his clipboard beside Nora's purse. "I'm tied up here. You should have called. I could have saved you a trip."

"It was on my way home." She shrugged. "Speaking

of trips, when are you two going camping? Surely Abby and Kimmie have had enough training. It didn't take this long to train and mobilize the troops for D-Day."

"Soon," Riley said vaguely.

"That was certainly definite." Her gaze slid from him to Abby. "Are you sure I can't talk you into dinner? Maybe Abby could join us?"

"I'd love to," Abby said. "But I have to pick up Kimmie from day care and we have a date to walk around the park track."

"Riley?"

He shook his head. "Maybe another time, sis."

"Okay, then. I'll see you tomorrow at the office. Bye, Abby. Nice to see you again."

When Nora had gone, Abby took a deep breath. She was stunned by the encounter. Nora had implied that Abby was somehow insincere where Riley was concerned. Women want a man with a job to pay for the white picket fence? Abby had paid for her own picket fence when Kimmie's father had walked out because he hadn't wanted them. She didn't want another man and certainly wouldn't resort to trickery to make a relationship happen.

But Nora had said Riley had been hurt by someone. The day Kimmie had skinned her knee and they'd talked about kids, she remembered his darkly intense reaction to the questions. At the time, she hadn't known him well enough to judge if the topic was painful. But Nora had just told her he'd been hurt. By whom? No time like the present to find out.

She looked at him. "Who hurt you, Riley?"

"What are you talking about?" He met her gaze, and the barriers in his own were crystal clear.

"Nora didn't stop by to take you to dinner. She wanted to warn me to stay away from you."

"What?"

"She said you've been hurt before and you're not as tough as you look. If my feelings aren't sincere, I should back off."

He shook his head and struggled for a casual air, but a muscle in his lean cheek jumped as he clenched his jaw. "Ignore her. That's Nora sticking her nose in my business."

"Now she's made it my business," Abby pointed out.

"I'll talk to her—"

"No. Talk to me. What happened to you? Who hurt you so badly your sister feels the need to prevent it from happening again?"

"It's no big deal," he said.

"Oh? That is not the impression I got from Nora. She said something about single mothers who want white picket fences and fathers to pay for them. She lumped me in there. Since I'm taking the heat for your emotional baggage, I think it's a very big deal. The least you can do is level with me."

He looked at her for a long time, so long it seemed as if he wouldn't answer. Then he released a long breath. "I told you I was married before."

"And you're not now, which means you're divorced."

He nodded. "Barb was pregnant when we met. She was a civilian working on the base where I was stationed. The baby's father had walked away from his responsibility and I felt sorry for her. We got to be friends."

"And friendship turned to love?"

"She needed medical benefits and a name for her child. And I cared a lot about her."

"I see."

"Things were good after my son—after Sean was born." His face softened for a moment, then the tender expression vanished. "For the next two years, life was good. I had a family. I can't remember a time I was happier. And I thought Barb was, too."

She remembered the way he'd looked when she'd asked him about his past. She recognized the same expression now—the deep lines beside his nose and mouth, the shadows in his blue eyes, the straight line of his mouth. He was remembering sadness and loss.

"What happened?" she asked.

"I couldn't have loved that boy more if he'd been my own child. Finally I understood that my adoptive parents could sincerely care about me even though I wasn't their own flesh and blood." It was as if now that the dam had been opened, everything was spilling out of this normally reserved man.

"What happened?" she asked again.

"The boy's biological father came back. He wanted his son, and Barb decided it was important for the boy to know his real father. I found out that love is no match for the right DNA."

Abby put her hand on his arm, not sure if he needed the comfort so much as she needed to give it. "I'm so sorry, Riley."

He shrugged as if that was that, but didn't pull away from her touch. "Don't be. It's ancient history."

Abby knew better. Her heart hurt for this man, so strong on the outside, so tender where it counted. At the same time, she remembered what Nora had said about her brother being happy lately. Was it possible she and Kimmie were a replacement for the family he'd lost?

Abby let that thought sink in. She was wildly attracted to him—even more since the night of the dinner and that spectacular kiss. But what if he were simply substituting them for what he couldn't have? Or worse. What if it was all about pity? Now she realized that a man who took too much on his shoulders and tried to rescue the world could be worse than a man who walked away from his responsibilities. She didn't want his pity.

"Do you ever see your—the boy?" she asked.

He shook his head. "I thought it best to stay out of the picture, not confuse him."

He loved the child enough to not be a part of his life. Abby was angry with the woman who'd hurt this really good man.

He sighed and picked up his clipboard. "I'm sorry Nora interfered. I'll talk to her—"

"No." If there was one thing she could understand, it was the need to protect the ones you love. She admired his sister for that. "She was just trying to help. I'm not upset." Not about that, at least.

"Good."

"And I think she's right about one thing."

"It always makes her happy to be right," he said.

"It's time we take the camping trip so Kimmie can get her badges."

He frowned. "Are you sure the two of you are ready?"

"Yeah. I am."

Nora had caught her just in the nick of time. It would

be a disaster to let her simmering feelings for Riley come to a full boil. Somehow she had to find a way to stop emotions that were growing stronger every time they were together. If she dragged on this survival training routine any longer, she wasn't sure she'd survive Riley Dixon. Fortunately, there was a simple solution.

They needed to do the campout before she didn't care that she might be no more than his latest charity project.

After their evening walk, Riley came inside with Abby and Kimmie. He stood at the bottom of the stairs and leaned on the railing as Abby told her daughter that they were going to do the campout over the next weekend.

Kimmie folded her arms over her chest and put on a stubborn face. "I'm not ready yet."

Neither was he. When Abby had said she wanted to get it over with, everything in him had rebelled. But he was a soldier. Throwing a tantrum was against regulations. "You'll do fine," Riley assured the little girl.

"I need more training. 'Member what happened the last time?" She looked at her mother, a pleading expression in her eyes. "My legs got tired, then I got tired breathing."

Abby squatted in front of the little girl. "You can make it this time because we have more stamina. If you're going to stay in Caitlyn's group, we've got to do it soon."

"We still have a little time. I'm not goin' yet and you can't make me."

"There's nothing to worry about, Kimmie," he said. "I'll be there and I won't let anything happen to you."

Her eyes filled with tears before she turned and stomped up three stairs. Then she stopped and glared over the railing. "I'm not changin' my mind. And that's final."

She stomped the rest of the way up the stairs and disappeared just before a door slammed on the second floor. Riley let out a breath. "Do you think it would help if I remind her that soldiers don't question a direct order?"

"No." Abby met his gaze. "It's not about orders or physical fitness or even fear."

"Then what is it about?"

Abby clutched her hands together as she glanced up, shadows in her eyes. "Did you see the look on her face when you said you'd be there? She's getting attached to you."

How could she know that based on a look? World peace would be easier to achieve than understanding the female mind at any age. In spite of his confusion, the thought pleased him. Because he was getting attached, too.

He'd figured that out when he realized he was inventing excuses to stop by and see them. Them—daughter and mother. It wasn't just Kimmie. Abby had a way of creeping into his thoughts at the damnedest times. Talking to clients. Mapping out security plans. Shaving. Showering. Sleeping. All thoughts led back to Abby.

"I don't understand," he said. "She's upset because I'll be there?"

"Kimmie knows when the campout is over, so is her physical fitness training. It will be time to say goodbye to you."

"That's not necessarily true," he pointed out. "We're friends."

"Oh?" She walked into the kitchen, then turned to face him when he followed. "You kissed me and I kissed you back. What do you call that?"

"Friendly."

"You know what I mean," she said.

"I do. And if you're worried because of what Nora said about single mothers and picket fences, don't be. She didn't mean it."

"I'm not worried. And yes, she did."

"Look, as far as I'm concerned what happened is in the past. You don't have to prove anything to me."

"It's not you I'm worried about. It's my daughter. She's just a little girl."

"I'd never hurt her," he said.

"Not intentionally," she agreed. "But you can't make promises, either. And I don't want you to. I don't trust promises, from you or anyone else."

Riley studied her, the troubled expression on her face. Earlier, when he'd told her about his past, she'd touched him. That simple gesture of comfort had lifted the heaviness around his heart. He'd needed the connection and been grateful for it. Somehow, the pain of the past had brought them closer, but only for a moment. Then Abby had said they needed to get the trip over with. So who was really getting attached to him?

"And you're not concerned about yourself?" he asked.

"I can take care of myself. I'm a big girl."

And didn't he know it. Her kiss had packed enough firepower to give new meaning to a shock and awe campaign. "Don't tell me this isn't about what Nora said—"

"Your sister is concerned about you. And you should be grateful for that."

"I am, but—"

"She made a lot of sense. Basically her message was fish or cut bait. Since I'm not interested in fishing…" She shrugged.

"Nora doesn't know what she's talking about," he said, anger swelling through him. He needed to have a chat with his little sister.

"Yes, she does. The thing is, my feelings are sincere. I'm sincerely not interested in a personal relationship. Once was more than enough disappointment for a lifetime. For me and for Kimmie."

What the hell was he doing? This was what he'd wanted from the beginning. Complete the mission and slip away.

"So you think Kim is really ready?" he asked, pulling himself back from the brink. "For the trip, I mean?"

"Yes. And in spite of her tantrum, I think delaying any longer will only make it worse when we say goodbye to you." She folded her arms over her chest. "I'm making an executive decision. Damn the torpedoes, full speed ahead. We're doing the trip this weekend."

"Your mind is made up?"

"Absolutely," she said with complete conviction.

He leaned his elbows on the island between them, grateful that it was there. It reminded him *not* to take her in his arms the way he wanted to. "Do you ever worry about being wrong, Abby? I mean, when you make up your mind about something regarding your daughter?"

"Every day. But I wasn't given a choice about raising Kimmie alone. Any more than you were given a choice about not being included in raising Sean."

"Yeah."

"I didn't say that to hurt you. Just to make you understand that I have to put one foot in front of the other. I have to trust my instincts and hope for the best. The alternative is to be immobilized where she's concerned, and that's not an option."

"So there are times when you'd rather not be alone to parent her?"

"Every day," she said again.

"Would you rather her father came back?"

"For my sake, no. But for Kimmie…" She sighed. "Ideally, kids have two parents. The result is an even-handed upbringing. But it only works if the parents love each other, too."

Riley thought about his own situation: the chip on his shoulder because his own mother had walked out on him, his adoption and the doubts about acceptance in the family. But there'd never been any question that the Dixons loved each other. After briefly having a son, he'd understood how much they loved him, too. He always knew he'd been lucky to have a home, but now he realized the importance of love in giving that home stability.

He thought about Abby, questioning whether or not his friendship with Barb had evolved into love. He wasn't sure. Which made him wonder if they would have lasted even if Sean's father hadn't come back. He'd cared about that boy, and he cared about Kimmie. He'd told the truth when he said he'd never hurt her. Letting her get even more attached would do just that.

Abby was right. It was time to do this and walk away. Before they got in too deep. Or at least any deeper, he thought, remembering the tears in the little girl's eyes.

She'd been hurt, and so had Abby. He didn't want to hurt them any more and he couldn't make the past go away. He was damaged goods and no good to them.

"Okay," he finally said. "I see your point and we'll go with the executive decision. I'll pick you and Kimmie up Saturday morning."

"Same as last time? Oh-dark-thirty?" she asked with the ghost of her familiar grin.

"Yeah." He did his best to grin back. "But it's your job to convince Kimmie to go along with the program."

"Just leave it to me."

Leave—so many meanings to a soldier. It was the chance to go home and see loved ones; it was tearing himself away again. He didn't like taking his leave of Abby and Kimmie. But he was grateful for the reminder that caring too much could cost him everything. Again.

This time when he walked out of her house, he didn't look back to see if she was watching him leave. He already knew what a temptation that was. He'd given in to it once and wasn't sure he could resist if faced with the temptation again.

As he drove away, he waited for relief to wash over him. Their association was almost over. But all he felt was a deep and profound emptiness in his gut.

So much for not being in too deep.

Chapter Eight

"So," Abby said, straightening the place mat hand-made by her daughter. She'd drawn three stick people and one didn't need to be a shrink or an art buff to know it was Kimmie, Abby and Riley. She covered it with her paper plate and muffin. "Are you excited about the camping trip tomorrow?"

"I guess." Kimmie picked at her own muffin, then took a sip from the boxed apple juice provided by the first grade room mother.

Muffins With Mom was a function designed to involve parents in school, to show the children how much the adults valued learning. Kimmie had brought home the announcement along with an RSVP; a head count was necessary to provide enough food. Along with the place mats, the children made name cards for their mothers. The tables and chairs, scaled down to accommodate six-year-olds, were arranged in a square in front of the teacher's desk. Personally, Abby liked the smaller size, but she was vertically challenged. How would someone like, say Riley, pour himself into it?

She would never know, but the mental image was priceless. Not so priceless was the fact that just casually thinking about him made her heart beat faster. The clear solution was not to think about him. Yeah, right.

"So, Kimmie, I like your classroom."

"But you've seen it before."

"I know. When you first started school." She glanced around at all the walls covered with artwork. "But Mrs. Nolet didn't have so much on the walls then. It looks really good."

With the juice straw in her mouth, Kimmie looked around. "I drew some leaves 'cause it's gonna be fall soon. It's over there," she said pointing to a bulletin board jam-packed with papers.

"Will you show me when we're finished eating?"

"Uh-huh." When she nodded enthusiastically, her bangs fell into her eyes.

Abby brushed the crumbs off her hands, then took her daughter's barrette and secured the hair. "There. That's better."

"Thanks, Mommy." She leaned against Abby. "I'm glad you're here."

"Me, too, sweetie."

"I'd be sad if you couldn't come." Her gaze rested on a boy sitting across the table from them. There was a place mat and card in front of the empty chair beside him. "Griffie is all alone."

"Maybe his mom couldn't come at the last minute."

"Yeah." Kim turned puppy dog eyes on her. "We should ask him to sit with us, Mommy."

Abby's throat tightened at the same time as she felt a sudden burning behind her eyes. How had she gotten so lucky? This tenderhearted child was a complete gift. In spite of her vow not to think about him, Riley popped into Abby's mind. Thoughts of the little boy who'd been abandoned by his mother tugged at her heart. He'd been adopted, but never quite felt he belonged. Then he'd found his own family, only to lose the child he'd come to love.

All of that explained why he hadn't put up more than token resistance when she'd said she wasn't interested in a personal relationship. But he was a warrior. She'd expected him to fight for what he wanted. Obviously he didn't want her, but she couldn't really blame him. When life kicked you in the teeth, you weren't likely to smile and give it another opportunity.

What a pair the two of them were, she thought. She'd also told him that her one and only relationship had been enough disappointment for a lifetime. In spite of her best efforts, she was in for more. She knew this because of her profound sadness at the thought of not seeing Riley after this weekend.

"Let's make room for Griffie," she whispered to Kim.

They scooted their chairs closer together, then she went with her daughter to move the little boy closer to them. When she had him settled, Mrs. Nolet walked over. The petite blonde looked frazzled. She pushed her wire-rimmed glasses up more firmly on her nose. "Thank you so much for taking Griffin to sit with you."

"It was Kimmie's idea," Abby admitted.

"His mother couldn't make it. So many moms work,

I knew not all of them could be here. That's one reason I needed the RSVP. To be forewarned so I could put kids without moms with the ones who were coming. But Griffin's mother didn't know until the last minute. I've been trying to find a moment to sit down with him, but it's been hectic."

Abby nodded. "I can only imagine. In the classroom setting, any change in the schedule can create chaos."

"That's for sure."

Abby glanced down at Kimmie, chattering away to the little boy who had finally smiled. "Don't worry about Griffie. He'll be fine with us. Just do your thing."

"Thanks."

As the teacher started to turn away, Abby stopped her. There'd been something bothering her ever since she'd received the Muffins With Mom notice. "Mrs. Nolet?"

"Yes?"

"Are you going to do a get-together with the dads?"

"In a few weeks," she confirmed. "Doughnuts With Dad."

"Very cute," Abby said, even as her heart squeezed painfully.

"I like it, too. Parent involvement is a key component in the educational process. But I don't have to tell you that. You're a teacher." She glanced around. "Please, excuse me. Now that everything seems to be under control, I've got to say a few words to thank the moms for coming."

"Of course," Abby said. "Don't let me hold you up. Griffie's in good hands."

"Thanks again."

She looked at Kimmie and wondered if anyone would make sure she didn't sit alone for Doughnuts

With Dad. Obviously, the teacher had tried to prepare for everything, but stuff happened. Abby knew the feeling. She'd bought Riley to do outdoor activities that she couldn't handle. An overnight campout. Nothing personal. Now Abby couldn't get the guy out of her head no matter how hard she tried. Five minutes ago, she'd promised herself she wasn't going to think about him, yet here she was thinking about him.

Well, she'd learned to be self-sufficient. She could do anything if she set her mind to it. Probably that would be easier when she wasn't in a heightened state of anticipation at the prospect of spending the weekend with him in a tent. Her. Wimpy umbrella-drink girl was actually looking forward to the campout, but she knew it was all about being with him, not the location.

Once the camping trip was done, so was she. Done with all things Riley Dixon. When she restored optimum mental function, the message might get from her brain to her heart.

It wasn't Doughnuts With Dad, but fishing with a friend was good, too.

Abby watched Riley and Kimmie by the stream and couldn't help thinking it was a Kodak moment. This trip was completely different from the last one. The hike in from where they'd left the SUV went off without a hitch. Carrying packs hadn't been a problem. No stamina or blister issues either. Camp was pitched—or whatever it was called when tents were erected with sleeping bags unrolled inside. Wood had been gathered for a fire and the place was as homey as one could make it in the wilderness.

The time Riley had spent preparing them made all the difference. If only there was some sort of decompression, debriefing or training that would make it easier to say goodbye. Fish or cut bait... They were fishing now and soon it would be time for the cut bait part. Sadness tightened in her chest.

No. She wasn't going there. She was going to enjoy this spectacular day in early November. But this was Texas where the saying went, if you don't like the weather—wait a minute. Right this minute, Abby sat in the foldaway nylon chair Riley had pulled from his pack and looked at the clear blue sky, sighing with pleasure. Who knew there was anything to like about backpacking?

Then she looked at Riley. Correction: two good things about being outdoors.

He was on one knee by the stream showing Kimmie how to bait the hook on her fishing line. When the child had shrieked in horror at all things slimy, he'd patiently worked with her until she'd accomplished the task instead of doing it himself, which would have been so much easier. Then he'd demonstrated casting the line as far out into the stream as possible. Over and over again he'd shown her and she wasn't even working for a badge in fishing. This was simply extracurricular outdoor stuff. If patience was a virtue, Riley Dixon was the most virtuous man on the planet.

Well, not entirely, she thought, shivering at the memory of his kiss. But at a moment like that, virtue could be highly overrated. She had to stop thinking that way. She had to put up her shields and get through this because... Why?

After today they wouldn't have any reason to see

each other. He wouldn't get personal because of his past. Just her luck to meet a great guy who had less reason to trust than she did. And just in case he did decide to take a chance, she would put on the brakes. She wasn't willing to risk that he wasn't substituting her and Kimmie for the family he'd lost.

Bottom line: they were two people with good, solid common sense where love was concerned. Neither of them was interested. There was no reason she couldn't simply relax and have a good time. Enjoy the enjoyable company of a man. By golly, she'd bought and paid for him; she was going to do just that.

Suddenly Kimmie started squealing and Abby's mom radar clicked on. She jumped up and ran to the edge of the stream. "What's wrong?"

"Mommy, I've got a bite."

"What? An insect? Snake?" She searched the area around them for slithery stuff.

"Fish," Riley said, obviously amused. "She's got a fish on her line."

"Oh, my gosh."

"Riley? What do I do?" Kimmie asked, holding her fishing pole with both hands to keep it from getting away. "Help me."

He squatted, sort of surrounding her, ready to take over if necessary. "Brace the grip of the pole against your tummy and hold it there while you turn the crank handle with your other hand. Bring him in closer and I'll get him in the landing net."

Shading her eyes with her hand, Abby looked at the stream current. She could see a fish jumping out of the water, struggling against the line. She wasn't sure she wanted anything to happen to the fish, but she was rooting for Kimmie's success. Talk about conflict. But she'd bought herself an expert. Let Riley deal with it, she thought.

Slowly, carefully and with as much concentration as a six-year-old could muster, Kimmie reeled her fish in close enough for Riley to net the creature. When he had it, Kimmie dropped the fishing pole and stared down at the fish struggling to survive.

Looking doubtful, she stared at Riley. "Did I hurt 'im?"

"No. But he's not happy."

"Is his family gonna miss him? Like Nemo's daddy when he couldn't find him?"

"It's a movie," Abby explained. "When Nemo is captured by fishermen, his father swims to the rescue."

Riley glanced at her, then finally said, "I guess his family will miss him."

Kimmie looked at the line protruding from the fish's mouth. "Is he gonna die?"

"If he stays out of the water too long." Carefully, as if he knew what was coming, Riley removed the hook from the fish's mouth.

"I don't want him to die."

"If we needed him for dinner, we'd have to," Riley gently explained to her.

Gravely serious, Kimmie met his gaze. "Do we have other stuff for dinner?"

"Yes."

"Can I put him back?"

"He's your fish."

"Even if I was hungry, I wouldn't want to keep him." Kimmie took the net from him and tipped it over the stream to let the fish go. When the creature became en-snared in the net's webbing, he helped dislodge it. Fi-nally, it disappeared beneath the water's surface.

Abby shaded her eyes against the sun's glare. "That's the luckiest fish in the Lone Star state."

"A new lease on life. I'm sure he'll make something of himself with his second chance." Riley grinned.

Kimmie was looking doubtful again. "I wish I could have brought my cereal."

Riley touched her nose. "Don't worry. I've got it all under control. You're not going hungry tonight."

She threw her arms around his neck. "Good. Be-cause I'm gettin' pretty hungry right now and it's not even night."

"Me, too." Abby figured it was all the fresh air and exercise, but suddenly she was ravenous.

"Then let's get dinner going," he agreed.

The kindling, prepared and surrounded by stones, was situated in an open area free of overhanging tree branches. Riley had long wooden matches and after lighting one, he handed it to Kim to ignite the fire. Abby watched Kimmie carefully, as did he, and both of them breathed a sigh of relief when it caught.

"I did it!" Kimmie said, excited about her success.

Riley took the wooden match from her and extin-guished it. "Yes, you did. Good job, kiddo. Now I'm going to clean—"

Abby cleared her throat loudly and when she had his attention, discreetly shook her head. "I'll help you get dinner ready."

"Understood." He nodded, indicating he got her hint about discussing dead fish in front of Kimmie.

"Can I help with dinner, too?" she asked.

Riley thought for a moment. "You can get water."

After he handed her a container, she trotted happily down to the stream.

Riley watched until Kimmie was out of earshot. "Sorry. I almost blew it."

"No problem. You redeemed yourself big-time sending her for water. That was a stroke of genius. She'll play for a long time with rocks and water."

"Yeah. I thought it would be some good, clean fun."

And so much more, Abby thought. His kid instincts were so good, so natural. He gave of his time. She thought about the woman who'd made him feel that he wasn't good enough. Abby wasn't prone to violence and always reminded Kimmie to use words to express her feelings. But somehow words weren't enough to express her outrage for what had happened to Riley. She wished for five minutes alone with the witch—no holds barred.

He pulled out a knife with a gazillion little tools stuck into the dividers. When he noticed her questioning look, he said, "Swiss Army knife. Don't leave home without it."

Abby watched him. "That's particularly nasty-looking," she said, when he started working with a serrated blade.

"This takes off the fish's skin and scales. After I fry it up in a pan, Kimmie will never recognize Nemo, his father or any other relatives."

"For the sake of her psyche and future good mental health, I hope you're right."

"Plus I've got MREs just in case we didn't catch any fish."

"Define MRE."

"Meals ready to eat," he explained.

"If one of them isn't a dehydrated hot dog, you're going to wish we'd lugged in that box of cereal."

When he laughed, Abby noticed the way the lines around his eyes crinkled. She watched him work, the competent, confident movement of his hands and the way the muscles moved beneath the tanned skin of his strong forearms. In that moment, she felt completely safe and absolutely content. And happy. If only it were possible to freeze this moment in time and stay here forever.

The rest of the evening was just as perfect. As the sun went down, they sat around the fire eating. After Abby told her it was "chicken," Kimmie tried the fish and pronounced it not too yucky. Because there was no TV and she was worn out from all the exercise and fresh air, she was soon tucked into her sleeping bag sound asleep.

Abby left her in the tent and felt the chill in the air before she went to sit by Riley in front of the fire. He was using the corkscrew from his Swiss Army knife on a bottle of wine.

"Where did that come from?" she asked, surprised.

"My backpack."

"That pack is like Mary Poppins' carpetbag—bottomless and magic."

"Just the necessities," he said, the fire glinting off his teeth when he grinned.

"So wine is a necessity and cereal is—"

"Empty calories."

"Ah," she said, gratefully accepting the plastic cup of chardonnay. "Perfect with fish. And the ambience…"

She glanced up at the spectacular sky filled with a gazillion twinkling stars.

"Perfect." The single word was spoken in a husky voice. When their gazes collided, she saw the dark intensity in his.

Suddenly, Abby felt more sparks between them than a campfire fanned by the wind. Certainly his Swiss Army knife had just the right tool to cut the tension. But she couldn't take a chance. It was time to take the heat off.

"So," she said, after several sips of wine. "Tell me about your life postadoption. What did you mean when you said you finally understood how your parents felt about you?"

"Where did that come from?"

She shrugged. "We're in the middle of nowhere, so the appropriate response would be—out of nowhere."

He stared at her for several moments and she suspected he knew exactly what the question was about. After resting his forearm on his upraised knee, he said, "I was four when my mother left and never came back, but I vaguely remember it. Trauma is like that, I guess. A single moment frozen in your mind forever. Then my parents came along. They didn't think having their own kids was in the cards, so they 'chose' me. It was scary, but they gave me lots of attention. And I had two sets of grandparents doting on me."

"Sounds awesome."

"It was. Until Nora."

"She put a crimp in your style?"

"Suddenly it felt like no one had time for me." He sipped his own wine. "I was grateful to be out of the orphanage, to have a family, but I didn't feel quite a part of it."

"Raising a baby is a twenty-four-hour-a-day job. Things were bound to change."

"Things definitely changed."

"Think back," she said. "As Nora got older, didn't things lighten up? Didn't your parents come to your sports events? Didn't someone show up for Muffins With Mom?"

"Huh?"

She shook her head. "School activities. The point is, your mom and dad probably had more time to split between you and Nora as she got older, when the needs of an infant eased."

"It's true. And that's what I meant when I said I realized how my folks felt. I got hands-on experience with a demanding infant, not to mention firsthand knowledge of how easy it is to love a child not biologically your own."

"That boy was lucky to have you, Riley, even for a short time. If you'd been his biological father, you wouldn't have walked out on him at all. Ever."

"For all the good that did me."

"Oh, Riley—" She remembered the look of profound sadness on his face when he'd talked about losing his family because his DNA was wrong. "You're plenty good enough," she said, emphatically. "Your sister would have been the one to feel the heat of your resentment and obviously she didn't. Because you're a wonderful, decent person. Nora thinks the sun rises and sets on you."

Automatically she reached out and rested her hand on his arm only to feel instant heat. He felt it, too, and his gaze turned hot, starting a fire in her belly. He put his cup of wine on the ground and set hers beside it. She'd have to be an idiot not to know he was going to kiss her.

This time, there was nowhere to run, even if she wanted to. And, God help her, she didn't want to. They only had tonight and she wanted it to be all that it could be. She wanted the rush, the heat in her blood from a single, isolated dangerous deed. She yearned for the excitement of not looking before taking the leap. She craved the thrill of testing the depth of the water with both feet.

But most important, she felt as if she would shrivel up and blow away—or worse, have major regrets—if she didn't kiss Riley Dixon.

He cupped her face in his big hands and she forgot to breathe. Then he touched his mouth to hers and her breathing went from zero to hyperventilation in half a second. He tasted of wine and wonder, and for several seconds she savored the sweetness of his soft lips. Heat wavered through her from the first brushing of their mouths and shimmered all the way to her toes. Suddenly she didn't feel the cold any more.

When he traced the seam of her lips with the tip of his tongue, she parted and welcomed him inside. An erotic heaviness settled in her chest as their mouths mimicked the act of making love. Then he changed direction; he was a man of action, after all. And his mouth was hot on her neck as she nestled into his arms. She was warm as much from the fact that this man was holding her close as she was from his body.

He slipped his hand under her sweatshirt and her breath caught at the exquisite feeling of his warm palm spanning her back. The sensation of skin to skin made her yearn for—for everything. Then he slid his fingers around her ribs and skimmed his hand over her breast. The first contact was like lightning, followed by electricity zinging through her.

"Abby," he whispered against her hair, as he teased her nipple to arousal through her bra. "You're so beautiful."

"No, I—"

"Yes, you are. You're beautiful and I want you." He shifted his weight, then grunted and reached behind him to move something out of the way.

It was Kimmie's princess backpack, and the equivalent of a cold shower. This was the wrong time and the wrong place. If her daughter weren't sleeping in a tent just a few feet away, she would give Riley anything he wanted. Without question. Or regret. He could have her—mind, body, soul. But it would only be one night, and that would be a mistake.

"I can't, Riley." She drew in a shuddering breath as she slid away. "I'm more sorry than I can say. But I can't."

"I'm sorry, too." He raked his fingers through his hair and sighed. "More than you can possibly know." He traced a finger over the backpack's pink handle. "But I understand."

She nodded. "I think I better say good-night."

"Yeah."

Before she could change her mind and stay with him, Abby went into the tent and slid into the sleeping bag beside her daughter's. In the dark, she listened to Kimmie's steady breathing and replayed what had just happened. The man knew his way around a kiss better than he knew his way around the outdoors. But the truth was that she and Riley could never have more than tonight because he didn't want to take a chance any more than she did. Although, more and more, that wasn't entirely true in her case, based on her all-consuming reaction to his kiss. Clearly their association was ending in the nick of time. Then again, she'd thought that before.

But this time, she really meant it.

Chapter Nine

"Where's Kimmie tonight?" Molly asked.

"At my folks'. As usual," Abby added. She and her friends had girls' night out often. Her parents loved taking their granddaughter, and Kimmie was treated like a princess for real.

She hadn't seen her friends since the auction and was anxious to find out what was going on with them. So here they were at the Nuthouse. It was booths, beer and beer-battered shrimp.

"Okay. Abby, you bought Riley at the auction," Charity said. "Actually, if memory serves, you bought two guys. What's up with you and Des O'Donnell?"

Abby met Molly's gaze, and the redhead shook her head slightly. "I'm not at liberty to say. But I can tell you that Riley fulfilled his commitment."

"That sounds interesting. And?" Charity stared expectantly.

"And—nothing." Abby heaved a big sigh.

"That is not the face or body language of a woman to whom nothing has happened," Jamie said. "I know this because as an attorney I study juries to decipher their verdict."

Abby knew there would be no peace if she didn't give them something. "Okay. He took us hiking and we camped out last weekend so Kim is officially eligible for her Bluebonnets badges. End of story."

Beside her, Molly half turned. "That big sigh moments ago and your Gloomy Gus face since we walked in here say there's more to this story. Give it up, Ab."

"You spent the night with him?" Charity asked.

"Outdoors. As in dirt, hard ground, cold, tent and sleeping bags."

"As in stars, clear sky, romance," Charity added.

"He did pull a bottle of wine out of his magic backpack and open it with the corkscrew on his Swiss Army knife."

"My kind of man," Charity said.

"Did he kiss you?" Jamie asked suspiciously.

"Why would you think that?" Abby hedged.

"Come on, Ab. Wine?" Jamie prompted. "I know he did because if he didn't, you would have simply said no."

"Is he a good kisser?" Charity demanded. "And don't edit out the good stuff. Tell us like it is."

Abby should have known her friends would wring every last detail out of her. "The man has a mouth and he knows how to use it."

"Then what's the problem?" Molly took a peanut from the red plastic basket in the center of the table and cracked it.

"I would think a close encounter of the kissable kind would perk you up."

"The problem is that he's not my type."

"Tell that to your mouth," Charity said. "And your hormones."

"How is he wrong?" Jamie asked.

"He's the Marlboro Man and I'm *Trading Spaces.*" Abby ran her fingernail through the condensation spot on her paper place mat and ripped a hole in it. "He's physical fitness and I'm a couch potato."

"None of this is serious stuff," Molly said. "What's really bugging you?"

"I bought him at the auction because I'm not the outdoors type. Automatically that makes us diametrically opposed."

"And you know what they say about opposites attracting?" Charity offered.

"Attraction isn't everything," Abby countered.

"It's a darn good start," Molly said.

"We came together for a specific goal—Kimmie's scouting badges. Mission accomplished. Now we have no reason to see each other again."

Charity pushed her half-empty wineglass away. "No reason except this attraction between the two of you. It would be a shame to waste it."

"The real problem is trust," Abby said, thinking about the kiss they'd shared. And bad timing—or maybe good, she thought. If she'd been alone with him… "I'm not looking to make another mistake, and neither is Riley."

"Speaking as the person who handled your divorce, how do you know it's a mistake?"

"You should know, Jamie. Don't you remember

when I first approached him about the weekend I bought, and he tried to buy it back?"

"Oh. Right. I forgot. Things on my mind," Jamie admitted. "You wanted to sue Riley, as I recall."

"It all boiled down to the fact that he didn't want to be around Kimmie and me. Since then, I found out that he had a painful break-up of his own. The woman he married to give her baby his name went back to the baby's biological father. He really misses his family."

"Wow," Molly said. "So you're afraid even if he's ready to take another chance, that you're a replacement for the family he lost."

"Exactly," Abby said, ripping the place mat to shreds. "I'm glad someone finally sees my point."

Molly shook her head. "But I don't. At least not when you look like you lost your best friend."

"The problem is that he spent more time on us than I paid for. He set up a training schedule for physical fitness, showed us how to use the camping equipment—"

"Not to mention that you went to the Chamber of Commerce dinner with him." Jamie shrugged. "My folks mentioned it."

"So you got used to having him around?" Charity asked.

"Yeah," Abby said simply. Sadly.

"Then don't let go of him," Jamie suggested adamantly.

Abby stared at her in surprise. "This from my divorce attorney?"

"What can I say? It's my job to protect my client's welfare, but I still believe in happy endings."

"I'm not so sure," Abby said.

Charity shook her head. "You can't turn your back

on him, Abby. That's the easy way out. And you're quitting before you even get started."

Abby thought about why Riley had insisted on training them for camping. He didn't want Kimmie to learn the lesson that quitting is okay. "I don't know."

"Sure you do," Molly said. "He was hurt because he lost his child. If he's a good father, I'll bet he's probably good husband material, too. Unlike the man who walked out on you."

"And he's good to his sister," Abby volunteered helpfully.

"This guy's too good to be true," Charity said. "So it makes perfect sense that you would thumb your nose at fate and turn your back on him without giving him a chance."

Abby looked at each of her friends. "And here I was counting on you guys to reenforce my decision not to see him again."

"What are friends for?" the three of them said in unison.

Abby and Kimmie walked past the client reading a magazine in the Dixon Security waiting room and into the Dixon Security inner sanctum. She told herself she wouldn't be here if (a) her friends hadn't convinced her not to give up and (b) her daughter hadn't lobbied long and hard for a visit with Riley to talk to him about "stuff."

So here they were. And there he was, behind his desk.

Although she knew he'd been on the high school campus from time to time, she hadn't seen him since the camping trip. It had only been about a week, but it seemed like forever. He looked awfully good dressed in his usual working attire of jeans worn in all the most intriguing places and a long-sleeved white cotton shirt rolled to the elbows. His dark hair was neatly combed and the pleased expression on his face said he was glad to see them. There was also a sexy sparkle in his blue eyes and she wondered if he was remembering their kiss in the Texas moonlight. God help her it was never far from *her* thoughts.

"Hi," Abby said, wiggling her fingers in a small wave. "I'm sorry to barge in, but Kimmie wanted to see you. And she was relentless."

"It's okay. A very welcome surprise," he said, his gaze going dark and intense for a second. Then soft and tender when he looked at her child.

"Hi, Riley," Kimmie said, marching straight up to him.

"Hi." He sat behind his desk and pulled her onto his lap.

She touched his keyboard tentatively, then looked around at the desk, chairs, and pictures on the walls. This time, Abby could see they were photos of a younger Riley with his soldier buddies. Her throat went tight at the sight of the uniform and what it represented—putting his life on the line to keep his country safe.

"I like your office," Kimmie said.

"Thanks. Me, too. To what do I owe the pleasure of a visit from the princess?"

"She wanted to talk to you about stuff," Abby explained. "Then she has something very important to ask."

"Okay." He looked at Kim. "You have my undivided attention."

Kimmie cleared her throat. "I just wanted to show you the scar on my knee from my boo-boo."

He frowned as he studied the small leg in front of him. "Yup, definitely left a mark. Are you okay with it?"

The child nodded. "I think it's cool."

"Then it is. What else is on your mind?"

"Well, I asked my grandpa if he's older than Santa Claus."

Riley's mouth twitched, a dead giveaway that he was struggling to keep a straight face. "What did he say?"

"That Santa's older. But I'm not so sure. Do you know how old Santa is?"

"Nobody knows," he said, imitating her serious tone. "It's top secret."

"But what do *you* think?" she insisted.

"I don't know how old your grandpa is."

"How old is he, Mommy?" Kimmie asked, shifting her gaze for the first time.

When Riley was around, Abby felt like a fifth wheel. But she couldn't bring herself to mind. "He's sixty-five."

Riley nodded. "Okay. Now we have a starting place." He thought for a moment. "Santa looked the same when I was your age. Which means it took a long time for his hair and beard to turn gray."

"My grandpa has some gray hair. When he needs to shave, his whiskers are all gray."

"Do you remember when he wasn't gray?" he asked Abby.

"Yes."

He nodded. "Then it's my best guess that Santa is older than your grandpa."

"Okay," Kimmie said, as if his word was gospel.

"Is there anything else?"

"We need to leave, Kimmie. There's someone waiting to see Riley."

"I'm not done yet, Mommy. I got a couple more things."

"It's all right," he said. "I'll make it up to the client. What else did you want to run by me?"

"Well, I have a Bluebonnets meeting in…" she touched her lip as she thought. "How many days, Mommy?"

"Two."

"In two days. And I'm gonna get my badges for hiking and camping."

"Congratulations."

"Well, I was thinkin'…"

"Uh-oh," he teased, looking at Abby.

"I know. When she thinks, you can almost see the lights in downtown Charity City flicker from the power drain."

He laughed, then returned his attention to the little girl. "What were you thinking?"

"I was thinkin' maybe you might want to come see me get my badges."

"Well," he said, "I'm honored."

Abby felt the need to jump in. First, because she didn't want him to think she'd put her daughter up to this. She didn't need a child to troll for men. Second, she didn't want him to feel any sense of obligation.

"Riley, it's all right if you're busy. I had no idea this was part of the 'stuff' she wanted to talk to you about."

"I need to check my calendar." He looked at Kim with an expression of complete and utter seriousness etched on the features of his lean, handsome face. "Getting your badges is kind of like getting a medal when you're a soldier."

"It's important," Kimmie agreed.

He nodded. "A very big deal. You worked very hard."

Kimmie smiled. "You helped me. And I just thought you might like to see."

"I wouldn't miss it."

Kimmie threw herself against him and his arms came around her in a hug. Abby felt her throat grow tight for the second time in less than ten minutes. She could be in a major state of monthly hormones. Or, and she was afraid this was more likely, her heart was melting for this big, tough ex-soldier who was putty in the hands of a little girl.

Abby cleared the emotion from her throat. "Okay, kiddo. We've taken up enough of Riley's time."

"But, Mommy, there's just one more thing."

"There's someone waiting, sweetie. We can come back another time—"

"It's okay, Ab. There's a lot of good reading material in my waiting room."

"I remember," she said wryly. "*Guns & Ammo* is pretty explosive stuff. Way more exciting than a good gossip magazine."

His mouth turned up at the corners before he returned his entire attention to her little girl. "Now, what else can I do for you?"

She scrambled off his lap and walked to Abby for her princess backpack. After unzipping it, she pulled out some paperwork. "My school is selling wrapping paper and ribbon and stuff. A lot of it's for Christmas. It's a fund-raiser and if I sell the most, I get the best prize."

"What is it?" he asked.

She frowned. "I don't remember. But it's good."

Abby sat down in one of the chairs in front of his desk. "I feel like the world's worst mom. Again, I had no idea she was going to hit you up. This is the first I heard about a fund-raiser."

"It's okay. I'll take one of everything," he said, looking at the order form. "Do you take checks?" he asked Kim.

"Yes," she said, nodding happily.

"But, Riley," Abby protested, "you don't seem like the wrapping-paper-and-ribbon type."

He met her gaze and amusement glittered in his eyes. "What? You think I don't celebrate the holidays?"

"It's not that. I get this really weird visual of you and ribbon and scissors and it's just wrong."

"The stuff will get used," he said. "Between Nora and my folks…"

"If you're sure," she said doubtfully.

"I'm sure." He looked at Kim, then met Abby's gaze with a sudden warmth in his own. "I have a feeling it's going to be a great Christmas."

"Yeah." Abby could hardly breathe. "This kind of explains where the Santa questions came from."

Leaving the amount blank, he wrote a check and gave it to Kim. "Let me know the total."

"I will," she promised, stuffing it in her backpack.

"Okay, now we really have to let Riley get back to work."

"Wait. Just one more thing," Kimmie pleaded.

"What is it?" he asked.

"Just before we went camping, Mommy came to my school for Muffins With Mom."

He glanced at her, then back to Kim. "I see." Clearly he didn't, but he patiently waited for her to continue. "Go on."

"My friend Griffie's mom wasn't there."

"Does he have a mom?"

"He does," Abby explained. "Mrs. Nolet, the teacher, asked all the parents to RSVP so she could step in for the kids whose parent couldn't be there. Griffie's mom had something come up at the last minute."

"He was sad," Kimmie explained. "So Mommy and me brought him to sit by us."

"That was very nice of you," Riley commented.

"Thank you." Kimmie blushed shyly at his compliment. "But…"

"What?" he prompted.

"Doughnuts With Dad is coming up. And I don't have a daddy. And I don't want to be sad, and I was just wonderin' if you'd come so I won't be sad." When the words stopped pouring out of her mouth, she slid a glance at him.

He looked at Abby. "Wow."

"I'm starting to sound like a broken record, but I had no idea she was going to ask you. Seriously, she won't be the only who doesn't have a dad there. And the teacher will make sure no one is left out. So you don't have to—"

"I'd love to go," he said to Kim. "Thanks for asking."

"You're welcome." The brightness of the smile on Kimmie's face could have illuminated the city for a month.

Abby's heart swelled with gratitude and something else she refused to even look at, let alone put a name to. "Thank you, Riley."

"No. Thank you," he said, first to her, then to Kim.

Suddenly his intercom buzzed and Nora's voice came through loud and clear. "Riley? I'm sorry to interrupt, but Mr. Milton is getting impatient."

Riley hit the respond button. "Okay. We're finished. Thanks, Nora."

He stood and walked them to the door, settling his hand on the knob. Abby knew her friends were right. Men like him didn't grow on trees and she'd be an idiot not to give this—whatever it was between them—a chance. After all, everyone knew you couldn't fool kids. And it was obvious that her daughter trusted him completely.

Abby took a deep breath and met his gaze, her heart stuttering at the expression in his eyes. "Since you're in the mood to say yes, I was wondering if you'd like to have dinner sometime? Let me say thank you for everything. I could cook—"

He touched a finger to her lips to stop her. "I'd like that. And I'll take you out."

"I'd like that," she said, echoing his words while her heart ceased stuttering and commenced a steady hammering against her ribs.

When he looked down, she noticed that Kimmie was tugging on his jeans to get his attention. "Riley?"

He squatted and looked her in the eyes. "Yes?"

She threw her arms around his neck. "I'm so glad you're coming to Doughnuts With Dad. Even though my daddy called."

"Your daddy called?" he asked, his voice cold, his gaze colder when he looked at Abby. "Don't tell me. You didn't know she was going to say that."

"I didn't. I had no idea she talked to her father."

"And I'm Santa Claus," he muttered as he straightened to his full height.

Without another word, he motioned the waiting client into his office. The door closed quietly, but Abby felt it all the way to her soul.

Chapter Ten

Abby tugged her daughter over to the chairs in the waiting room. "Kimmie, why didn't you tell me your daddy called?"

"I forgot." She rubbed her nose. "I just now 'membered."

"When did he call?"

"This morning."

"Where was I?"

"In the shower."

"What did he say?"

"He asked what I been doin'. I told 'im about The Bluebonnets and camping with Riley after you bought 'im at the auction. I told 'im about how Riley helped me catch a fish and the way he made my scrape feel better when he teached—"

"Taught," Abby automatically corrected.

"*Taught* me about first aid. I 'splained about how he

was training us so I could get my hiking badge. And that I'm getting my badges so Caitlyn and me can be together."

"What did your father say?"

She thought for a moment. "That he wanted to talk to you. I told him you couldn't come to the phone just like you always say to do."

"Did you ask for a phone number the way I always say, so I could call back?"

"Yes," she answered, nodding emphatically.

"Did you write it down?"

"No."

"Kimmie, remember what I told you?"

"He said he'd call back," she protested. "That's why I forgot. I didn't have to write anything down. And I was excited 'cause you said we could come and talk to Riley after school. I'm sorry, Mommy."

Abby gave her a half-hearted smile. "Me, too. But you did a good job, sweetie."

Boy, did she do a good job. If only she'd known, Abby could have brought it up in a kinder, gentler way. There was a very good reason six-year-olds didn't work in diplomacy.

Abby noticed that Nora was watching and listening— and made no attempt to conceal the fact that she was.

She looked at her daughter. "Kimmie, I need to talk to Nora. Do you have some homework in your backpack?"

"Yes." She pointed to the stacks of magazines on the coffee table. "But I wanna look at one of those."

"I think you're a little too young for *Guns & Ammo* or *Mercenary Monthly*."

"What's that?"

"It's for soldiers."

"Like Riley?"

No. Unlike mercenaries, he'd worked in military service defending his country because it was the right thing to do, not because he sold his services to the highest bidder. "I was kidding about that last one. But you need to start your homework. If you finish, you can look at a magazine."

"Okay." She slid so far back in the chair that her legs stuck straight out. Then she pulled her notebook and a pencil from her backpack and started to work on a math sheet.

Abby walked to the reception desk. "You heard?"

"Everything." Nora folded her arms over her chest.

"Cross my heart and hope to die, I had no idea Kimmie's father called."

"Yeah, I heard that, too."

She wasn't sure why, but it was vitally important for Riley's sister to believe her. "The man hasn't gotten in touch with me since the divorce and then all communication went through my attorney."

"You expect me to swallow this? He's had no contact with his daughter in all this time?"

"He signed away his legal rights to her because he didn't want to pay child support," Abby said, lowering her voice so Kimmie couldn't hear. There was no reason she should know how little her own father valued her. "If you don't believe me, I'll give you Jamie Gibson's office number. She's the attorney who handled everything for me."

Something flickered in the other woman's eyes and her expression softened. "Don't ask me why, but I believe you."

"It's the truth," Abby said. One Dixon down, one to

go. Relief made her knees weak and she sat down in one of the two waiting chairs. "Nora, I don't understand what just happened. I haven't seen Riley that distant since the first time I was in this office trying to collect my survival weekend."

"I remember." Nora looked uncomfortable.

"What?"

"Well…" She squirmed in her office chair. "There's no easy way to say this."

"Then just spit it out."

"You remind him of his ex-wife."

"I'm sorry I asked." Abby blinked. "Define 'remind.' I've never done anything like she did to him."

"No. It's a resemblance—hair, eyes, height—that sort of thing."

"Is that why he was so opposed to doing the weekend he'd donated?"

"Part of the reason," Nora confirmed.

"What's the other part?"

"He's afraid."

"Now I know you're making this up." Abby laughed, a tension reliever that was a dismal failure. "They say everyone has a twin, but I simply couldn't be that unlucky. And Riley's not afraid of anything."

"I'm not making it up. And Riley would kill me for saying this. But he's afraid of getting his heart broken again."

"So am I," Abby said. "But my friends made me see that sooner or later you have to take a chance, especially if you find a great guy like Riley. And one of my friends happens to be my divorce attorney."

"No, Abby. You don't understand."

"Enlighten me."

Nora leaned forward. "One of the things that made Riley such a good soldier was how much he loved it."

"The army?"

Nora nodded. "Specifically the Rangers. He was good at it. The discipline and adventure suited him. He'd found his niche, his career. Oddly enough, the same nobility, loyalty and sense of honor that made him such a good soldier were the same virtues that cost him that way of life."

"What do you mean?"

"He gave it up. For her."

"Why?" Abby felt a knot the size of Delaware form in her midsection.

"Soldiers are frequently away. Deployed to hot spots around the world, sent overseas for months at a time. That lifestyle is hard on families. And he wanted to be a husband to Barb and a father to the child he considered his. His career made the odds of domestic success slim, and he didn't want to take the chance."

"And she let him resign his commission? She went along with his decision to end such a promising career?" Abby couldn't believe it.

Nora nodded. "He gave up everything and she continued to take advantage."

"How?"

"When he decided to get out, he knew he needed a plan and decided the military training he'd received would complement a security business. And Charity City was just the up-and-coming place to set up his base of operations."

"How did Barb take advantage?" Abby glanced at

Kimmie and assured herself that her daughter was still occupied.

"I'm getting there. When he was around all the time, too often she left him with the baby while she went off and did whatever she wanted."

"At the same time he was trying to get his business off the ground?"

Nora nodded. "Then the biological father waltzes back into her life and just like that, she's outta there."

"She didn't care about Riley at all."

"Bingo," Nora said.

"She took everything from him—the career he'd worked so hard to build, the family he'd sacrificed everything for and the child he loved."

"The witch. If there wasn't a child within earshot, I'd substitute a B for the W in that word." Anger glittered in Nora's eyes. "She took it all without a backward glance. It was clear she never cared about him and simply used him as a meal ticket as long as she needed him. So you can see why he's gun-shy."

"Unfortunately, yes. And Kimmie's little bombshell was like déjà vu all over again."

"Right in one." Nora glanced over her shoulder at the closed door. "I'm not sure how long he's going to be tied up, but if you want to wait—"

Abby shook her head. "I have to get Kim home. But thanks."

"For what?"

"Explaining."

"You're welcome, I think."

Abby knew she had some explaining of her own to do. But now wasn't the time because Riley was with the client he'd kept waiting while putting her and Kim first. She'd talk to him at Kimmie's scouting meeting. That would give her an opportunity to make him understand a few things—such as that she hated resembling the woman who'd crushed his heart. But she wasn't that woman and her ex-husband may have called, but that didn't mean this was a repeat of what Barb had done to him. Abby had no intention of going back to the man who'd turned his back on her and his daughter.

With a plan in place, Abby smiled confidently at Riley's sister before ushering her daughter into the elevator. When they were alone, she remembered the dark look of betrayal on his face. The knot in her abdomen pulled tighter, and she knew it wasn't about the elevator car plunging toward the first floor.

It was all about convincing Riley she'd had no contact with her ex-husband and wouldn't take him back if he got down on his hands and knees and crawled all the way to the Panhandle.

Riley walked into the high school library for a quick look-see at the metal detector being installed there. Because it was lunchtime, most of the student body and faculty would be tied up in the cafeteria. But when his eyes adjusted from the bright sun outside, he saw Abby toying with a salad at her desk.

The sight of her was like a blow from a two-by-four to his midsection. She was so beautiful, it was almost painful to look at her. Because he didn't want to see her.

And he wanted to see her more than anything.

She'd kissed him back on that camping trip. No question about it, in his mind. He'd been so sure her breathless reaction and passionate response had been genuine.

And a few days ago, when Abby and Kimmie had come to his office, the future had never looked brighter. Kim, with her precocious questions and asking him to be there for her, counting on his support. Then Abby had shyly suggested dinner, indicating her shift in policy regarding something personal. And last, the bombshell when her little girl had mentioned the father who was supposed to be out of the picture. So Riley had gotten his teeth kicked in again. *And* by the same scenario. Once wasn't enough for him.

But now she was there looking at him and he had nowhere to go. Never a foxhole when you needed one. "Hi, Abby."

"Hi, yourself."

"I'm here to check out the new hardware," he said, cocking a thumb at the electronic archway.

"I guess you thought I'd be at lunch. You probably wanted to slip in and out—covert-style."

"I tried to pick a time that was the least disruptive to your students."

Not seeing her would have been less disruptive—at least to his pulse and heart rate. His body was still reacting as if she were the sweet innocent he'd thought her to be. The woman with no ulterior motives.

"So much for a clean getaway. I decided to eat lunch in here today." She stood and folded her arms over her chest, then leaned a hip against her desk. "Kimmie and I missed you at The Bluebonnets last night."

"Something came up." He didn't even pretend to

misunderstand the statement, but he concealed the wince when she mentioned Kim.

"Something came up," she said dryly. "Well, that certainly explains everything. Or is that what you say when you could tell me but then you'd have to kill me?"

He met her gaze and saw the anger snapping in her normally warm brown eyes. "I couldn't make it," he said vaguely.

"Still not clear. And buster, unless both your arms were broken, you don't have a good enough excuse."

"What does that mean?"

"You're in the security business," she said, lifting her chin toward the equipment he'd come to check. "You've got a passing acquaintance with gizmos. Surely you know your way around a cell phone. That's child's play for the *average* person."

He should have called. The fact she was right made him defensive. "I don't owe you anything."

"Not me. Kimmie. You owe her something. You gave your word. And if that's not bad enough, you broke a promise to a child—my child," she said, tapping her chest. "But therein lies the problem. It's because she's my child that you hurt her. Because you're angry with me. The least you could have done is give me a chance to explain."

"There's nothing to say." He folded his arms over his chest. "My obligation to you is fulfilled. Kimmie got her badge—"

"How would you know? You weren't there." She held up her hand. "I know. You couldn't make it. Look, Riley, just because I resemble your ex-wife doesn't mean—"

There was only one person who could have given her that information. "What did Nora tell you?"

"That because of your commitment to your family, you gave up your career. I know you lost everything when your wife went back to her baby's father."

"And your point?" he said, barely holding onto his temper. He'd been an idiot then. He was an even bigger one now because he should have known better, but he'd marched in—double time—with his eyes wide open. Time to take it on the chin like a man.

"My point is that it doesn't take a psychobabble expert to get that when you found out Kimmie's father called, for you it was like history repeating itself."

He looked around at the rows and rows of books. "Have you been spending too much time in the self-help section?"

"You should try it." She walked over to the counter, which was the only thing separating them, and looked him straight in the eye. "But you could read all the books in the world and it comes down to one thing— it's time to deal with it."

"Is that the pot calling the kettle black?" he challenged.

"It would have been. But that day I came to your office, I'd decided to get over it."

"I hear a *but*."

"You bet there's a *but*. You didn't bother to ask questions. You simply went to the bad place."

"Define bad place."

"That's where you assign me blame for something I haven't done. I had no idea Fred called. Whether or not you believe it, that's the truth. And I still don't know why he did because I haven't heard any more from him. Which is typical. And here's some more of my point. He turned his back on his own child. There's nothing he could say or do, now or ever, that would compel me to take him back after that. He violated a basic social and moral code, and it's unforgivable."

Hell of a time for him to remember she'd once told him he reminded her of her ex. "What does that have to do with me?"

"When I first met you, I jumped to the conclusion that you were like Kimmie's father because you had a few things in common." Her full lips tightened for a moment. "But everything you did said that you're noble, loyal, conscientious, caring. And I felt like a jerk."

"Look, Abby, it's been a long time since I thought about any resemblance. I'm not judging you—"

"Yes, you are and you came to the wrong conclusion. But I'm judging you, too. And I think my first impression was right after all."

"What does that mean?" he said. Now she was hitting below the belt.

"Kimmie's father walked out on her. You're doing the same thing."

"Now wait a minute—"

"No," she said, pointing at him. "I'm all my daughter has. If I don't look out for her, who will? I won't let you or anyone else get away with treating her badly. She's just a child. She's hurt and confused because of you. The worst isn't that you're just like Fred The Flake. The worst is that you made Kimmie think you were different. You made her care about you."

"I care about her, too."

"You have a funny way of showing it." She brushed the back of her hand across her cheek and took a deep breath. "But then, I should have expected it."

"Why?" He didn't know why he asked because he knew he wasn't going to like the answer.

"I was shocked and angry when my husband left and broke his promise to come back. But that's nothing compared to what I feel now."

"Which is?"

"I hate myself. I'm the worst parent in the world. I brought another man into our lives and my child has suffered because of it. And—"

She walked out from behind her counter and headed for the door.

When she started to pass him, he reached out and curled his fingers around her upper arm to stop her. "And what, Abby?"

She met his gaze and her own was glistening with unshed tears. "And I did what I said I'd never, ever do again. I fell for you." She drew in a shuddering breath. "But I've learned to live with disappointment once. I can do it again."

Chapter Eleven

Riley walked into his office to find Nora checking his calendar against a computer printout. "Good morning," he said.

"Is it?"

"Yes?" he said hesitantly, hoping it was the right answer.

Personally, he hadn't had a good morning—or night, for that matter—since he'd found out Abby's ex-husband had called. He sat down behind his desk.

"Why do you look like you're getting ready to work?" she asked.

"I own the company?" he replied questioningly.

She pointed to a hastily scribbled note on his desk calendar. "What's DWD, and don't even try to tell me it's something to do with the Defense Department."

"Driving while dysfunctional?" he tried.

"If that were true, no one would even be eligible for

a license," she pointed out. "Everyone I know suffers from varying degrees of dysfunction. We all have idiosyncrasies tending toward lunacy." One of her eyebrows lifted, followed by a piercing look that meant she was going to make a point and he wouldn't like it. "But for the record, I'd like to say that some of us have more degrees of dysfunction than others."

He glanced at his scribbled note. "Look, it's just letters. I was doodling."

"Uh-huh." She traced something else on the calendar. "And tell me these initials—A and K—inside a heart stand for that rifle thing."

"I assume you're talking about an AK-47. You know how I feel about them—"

"Don't split hairs, Riley. What in the blazes does it stand for?"

Why did he even bother to try and sidetrack her? And he didn't bother pretending he didn't know what "it" she meant. "DWD means Doughnuts With Dad."

"I'm going to take a shot in the dark here and guess it has something to do with Kimmie?"

He nodded. "School function."

"And why is it on your calendar?" When he didn't answer right away, she put her hands on her hips and gave him the look again. "Don't bother to lie. I'll know if you are."

"I said I'd be there," he admitted. He'd outright promised, but he didn't want to phrase it that way.

"It's today."

"Yeah."

"So what are you doing here?"

"I'm not going," he said.

"But you promised."

So much for his cautious phrasing. "Look, Nora, it's complicated."

She nodded, but the penetrating look in her eyes didn't soften. "I can see how keeping a promise could be."

"Here's the thing. If I'm there, she'll get the wrong idea. It will just prolong the inevitable. If I don't show, she'll forget about me by lunchtime. At first, she might be disappointed—"

He remembered Kimmie's face when she talked about learning to live with disappointment. How many times could you knock a kid down before they stopped getting back up? He felt lower than a snake's belly.

"Yes?"

"It's complicated, Nora. Leave it alone."

"I can't. Because this isn't about Kimmie. At least, not in a direct way. It's about Abby, making it about you. That's where it becomes my business."

"What about Abby?"

"I'm going out on another limb here. This situation with her isn't like with Barb."

"And you know this how?"

"I just do. She said she had no idea her ex-husband called until Kimmie blurted it out here. I, for one, believe her. She doesn't sound like a woman who's planning on getting back together with the guy."

"It doesn't matter."

"You're lying," she accused.

She was right, although he'd eat glass before admitting it. The truth was, Abby and Kimmie mattered a hell of a lot. More than he'd meant for them to matter.

In his gut, he knew he'd never loved Barb. He'd realized it when Abby had asked him if his friendship with Barb had grown into love. He'd liked her, but loved the idea of having a family. When they broke up, it was his son he'd missed—not Barb.

But Abby was different. She lived love every single day. She was there, doing the hard stuff. Putting one foot in front of the other because she loved her child more than anything. She ran interference for Kimmie and wouldn't let anyone dump on her because Abby cared with all her heart.

And Abby cared about him.

That was the last thing she'd said before he'd left her in the library over a week ago. That and the fact that she wasn't happy about her feelings. That he was worse than the man she'd divorced. And she'd learn to live with the disappointment. At the time, he'd thought she was wrong—that he was nothing like her ex-husband. Now he wasn't so sure. He'd let Kimmie down already and was about to do it again.

Since the day Abby had given him a piece of her mind, he'd thought about little else besides her. Somehow Abby, and Kimmie, too, had sneaked past his emotional perimeter. And he wasn't so sure he would ever learn to live with that disappointment.

"It doesn't matter?" Nora said, her voice rising an octave. "This from the man who still has the emotional scars because his adoptive parents had the audacity to conceive a child?"

"I'm so over that," he scoffed.

"Right. And I could see by the look on your face when Kimmie said her father called that you're over what Barb did to you."

"I am over it."

"Prove it. Go to that school function. Because the bottom line is you're a grown man. Kimmie is a little girl. If you think your behavior isn't going to scar her for the rest of her life, then you're a five-star general in charge of fantasyland."

Speaking of giving a piece of her mind, Nora was really on a roll, he thought. And she didn't know he'd already stood Kimmie up once already. He felt like a by-product of nuclear waste sludge for what he'd done.

"I don't know how to respond to that."

She put her hands on her hips. "Fortunately, you don't have to because I'm not finished with you yet. You're a lying weasel dog. A coward."

"Am not." He tried to smile, to draw her into their childhood give-and-take. But they weren't children any more and the look on her face said she wasn't going there.

"I don't mean 'fraidy cat in the traditional sense," she went on as if he hadn't spoken. "There's not a doubt in my mind that you'd take a bullet for anyone you loved."

"Damn straight," he agreed.

"And I think Abby and her daughter are at the top of your list. You'd march right into hell and spit in the devil's eye without flinching, but taking a chance on Abby scares the hell out of you."

"Who died and made you the resident shrink?" He'd meant to sound teasing, but there was a defensive edge to his voice. She was way too close to the target.

"You're a big chicken, Riley." She made chicken noises and moved her arms as if she were flapping wings.

"You know," he said, studying her. "Cupid has wings."

She shook her head. "Not me. No way. I don't like anyone messing in my love life. Pathetic as it is. But I'll tell you this. You can do what you think is right. You always have and always will because it's the way you're wired." She pointed at him again. "But—and I mean this with every fiber of my being—if you stand that little girl up for Doughnuts With Dad, I will personally break your kneecaps."

"You and what army?"

"Don't push it. I've got connections."

He was trying for flippant, but she shot him a glare on the way out of his office. He looked at the scribbling on his calendar and traced the heart he'd absently drawn around their initials. Was his subconscious trying to tell him something?

Or was it time to stop thinking too much? He'd been in a lot of tight spots and instinct had saved his life more than once. Maybe he should simply go with his gut on this one.

Abby watched her daughter from a glassed-in area just off the first grade classroom. She could see without being seen as dads arrived and sat with their children, just like Muffins With Mom day. Kimmie's hopeful gaze darted to the door every time it opened, and every time the man walking in wasn't Riley, the hope died.

The door to the hideaway room opened and Mrs. Nolet walked in. "Hi, Abby."

"Hi." Abby had explained that Kimmie's stand-in dad probably wouldn't be there and had received permission to wait in the wings if needed.

The teacher pushed her glasses up on her nose. "You know I won't let Kimmie be left out. If you need to get to work—"

Abby shook her head. "I took the morning off."

"Okay." She nodded and left, moving around the classroom, making sure the event was going smoothly.

Abby had tried to prepare her daughter for the fact that Riley wasn't coming, but the little girl refused to believe it. When he'd missed the Bluebonnets meeting, she'd made excuses—maybe he had been sick, or his car had broken down, like theirs had that time. Abby had explained that he'd fulfilled his auction obligation to them and now he was moving on, but her little girl wouldn't accept it. He'd promised. And it didn't matter a fig to her that he'd also promised to be at her meeting. She'd been adamant that on Doughnuts With Dad day, she wouldn't be sitting by herself like Griffie.

But Abby wasn't taking any chances. If no one invited Kimmie to sit with them, Abby would be there. It broke her heart that she couldn't be everything to her child. If she could, her little girl wouldn't even notice that men let her down on an annoyingly regular basis.

Abby saw Kimmie look toward the door and braced herself again for the look of disappointment. Instead, Kimmie's little face lit with animation, and she jumped up and waved. Following her gaze, Abby saw a man, slightly taller than the few who were milling around. He waved and squatted down as Kimmie raced over and then hurled herself at him, practically disappearing as he folded her into his strong arms.

Tears burned Abby's eyes as the little girl took Riley's big hand in her small one and led him to her six-year-old-sized chair. He looked questioningly at the identical empty seat beside hers, then lowered himself carefully. Kimmie laughed at the picture he made, with his knees practically touching his nose. No way would his long legs fit under the table. Most of the dads had the same problem, but not as bad as Riley.

Not only did he stand head and shoulders above the other men, he was by far the hottest guy in the room. Abby had the racing heart and sweaty palms to prove it.

Just then, Mrs. Nolet poked her head in. "He's here, Abby. Kimmie's not alone."

She started to answer and found her voice thick with emotion. After she cleared her throat, she said, "Yeah. I saw him come in."

"So if you need to go…"

"If it's all right, I'd like to stay and watch."

The blonde nodded. "No problem." She started to leave, then poked her head back in. "By the way, he's not hard on the eyes. Is it serious between you?"

Yeah, she wanted to say. A serious problem with serious pain because their pasts got in the way. "No."

"I'm not being nosy," she explained. Then she grinned. "Maybe just a little. But it's helpful to know if there are any big changes in a child's life. It can affect their ability to learn."

"I understand." Abby shook her head. "But he's just a friend. There won't be anything happening that will impact my daughter."

"Okay. Talk to you later."

Abby couldn't take her eyes off the two in the other room. She was entranced and charmed by Riley's easy manner with her daughter and the other men he chatted up. He exuded warmth and an innate caring for the children, none of whom were his own. Probably because he knew how it felt to not belong. Unfortunately, the woman he'd married had put him back to square one—on the outside looking in. Now Abby and Kimmie were paying the price for what she'd done.

Finally, it was time for the kids to go to recess and the dads to leave. Abby followed Riley to the school parking lot and watched him unlock his SUV with the keyless entry.

"Hi," she said.

He turned at the sound of her voice, but didn't look all that surprised to see her. "Hi."

"I just wanted to thank you for coming. It meant a lot to Kimmie." *And to me,* she thought. But he wouldn't want to know that.

"You don't have to thank me. I enjoy spending time with her." He rubbed his hand across the back of his neck. "About missing her meeting, Abby, I tried to apologize to her. But she was too busy showing me around her classroom. She's a terrific kid. Sorry isn't anywhere near enough. It's just that—"

She held up her hand. "You don't have to explain."

"I want to."

"I don't want to hear it."

"Okay. For now." His expression turned intense. "Do you want to hear how I feel about what you said the last time we talked?"

Heat crawled up Abby's neck and settled in her cheeks. Apparently it was too much to hope that he either hadn't heard or would choose to ignore her emotional confession. If she hadn't been so doggone upset about what he'd done to Kimmie, her guard would never have slipped enough for her to admit she'd fallen for him.

"It's no big deal, Riley. Just forget it."

"I don't want to forget it. I can't."

"I plan to." She huffed out a breath. It was time to change the subject and she knew just the thing. "There's something you should know."

"What's that?"

"Fred finally called me back."

"And?" His mouth thinned as a muscle contracted in his cheek.

"He wanted to give me a head's-up that an entertainment reporter would be calling me for an interview." With her hand, she shielded her eyes from the sun's glare and stared into eyes as blue and clear as the Texas sky. Big mistake. She cleared her throat. "Fred wants me to tell her that even though we're divorced, he's a terrific father who supports his daughter and me financially and emotionally. That we're terrific friends and parent our beautiful child together."

"In other words, lie. Except about the beautiful child part."

"Pretty much."

"So did you?" he asked.

"I don't lie. Ever," she said emphatically. Not about anything. Including her feelings for Riley, although that was the last thing she wanted to talk about. If she could rewind their last conversation and take back the words, she'd do it in a heartbeat. "The fact is, no one's called me to ask about him. It's Fred tilting at windmills again. I just thought you should know."

"Thanks for telling me."

"You're welcome. And again, thanks for coming today."

"You didn't think I would. That's why you're here, isn't it?" He held up his hand. "I don't blame you. Based on my recent unforgivable behavior."

"I just didn't want Kim to be alone. She has such a tender heart and—"

When her voice broke, Riley moved closer and touched her hand, took it in his own. The warmth felt so good wrapped around her fingers. How she would love to trust him, to take the support he was offering. But she couldn't trust and she had to stand on her own two feet. She'd made the mistake of reaching out to Riley once. She wouldn't do it again. Not only because she hated being needy, but it hurt too much when you loved someone who couldn't love you back.

"Abby—"

She pulled her hand away. "I have to get to work."

"Wait, we need to talk."

"I don't have anything else to say." She stepped up on the curb.

"I have plenty to say."

She walked slowly backward. "Now that camping is over, so are we. There's nothing you can say that I want to hear."

Because all she wanted to hear was that he loved her, and it was the one thing he couldn't say. She turned away before he could see the tears in her eyes and walked to her car as quickly as possible.

He was noble and loyal and wonderful, and he would try to do the right thing. But he obviously couldn't love her. It had been stupid to even hold out hope that he could. She was umbrella drinks and ordering off a menu. He was catch it, kill it, cook it over an open fire. The differences between them were why she'd bought him in the first place—to give her child what she couldn't. It was never supposed to get this personal.

She backed her car out of the space and looked in her rearview mirror. Riley still stood there, watching. Sweeping the back of her hand across her cheek, she brushed at the trail of tears. It hurt a lot to know this was the last time she would ever see him. Her heart cracked, and she was pretty sure she'd never be able to put it back together.

Because she'd never loved anyone the way she loved Riley.

Chapter Twelve

"But, Mommy, why can't I ask Riley to come over for dinner?"

Abby glanced in the rearview mirror at her daughter, securely buckled in the backseat. They'd just come from day care and were on the way home. Kimmie had chattered nonstop about her day at school, which included Riley and Doughnuts With Dad. How could she make this child understand that the man they'd both fallen in love with wasn't coming around anymore?

"It's not polite to bother him. He probably has plans, Kimmie." Now wasn't the time for that conversation, because Abby knew she was dangerously close to an emotional meltdown as it was. When it happened, she wanted to be in the privacy of her own bedroom where her little girl wouldn't see.

"Today at Doughnuts With Dad, he told me he wasn't doing anything tonight," Kimmie said.

"Did he volunteer that information? Or did you grill him like a raw hamburger?"

"Huh?" The little girl brushed her hair out of her eyes.

"Did you ask him a lot of questions?"

There was complete silence. Abby kept her eyes on the road as she asked, "Are you shaking your head? Use words, Kim."

"No. I didn't bother him. He just said so."

"Why would he tell you he didn't have anything to do tonight?"

"Because he wants me to call and 'vite him over for dinner. How many times do I have to tell you?"

One glance and Abby read her body language— hands out, palms up clearly saying *duh*. Kimmie was a miniversion of her, and the words were straight from Abby's top ten list of maternal rhetorical questions. If only her brain didn't seize up when irritation got the better of her and she could remember what a little sponge her child was. It was like looking into a mirror, and the reflection she saw wasn't pretty.

But right now, Abby was too focused on her own pain and loneliness to even be irritated. Surely Riley hadn't been hinting for an invitation. He'd shown up today because he felt badly about breaking a promise, but Doughnuts With Dad was his last obligation to them and he was moving on. She needed to do the same. And she would know she had when the thought of never seeing him again didn't produce a fresh wave of sadness and raw pain. Somehow she had to convince Kim to back off. Let it go. Let him go. Maybe that would be easier, Abby thought, when she figured out how she was going to forget him.

She turned onto their block, grateful that they were almost home. Neighborhood kids were playing ball in the street, and she drove slowly, watching that they were all out of the way.

"Mommy, what's that in our front yard?"

"What, sweetie?" She glanced at her house and for the first time saw what looked like a domed tent in the front yard. If she wasn't mistaken, it was the ultralight one they'd slept in on the campout.

"There's a bunch of kids in our yard," Kim said, pointing out the obvious.

They were gathered around the tent and a tall man beside it. Abby's heart started to hammer and the blood rushed to her head, pounding in her ears. The noise was so loud it took several moments before she realized what Kimmie had said.

"Mommy, that looks like Riley,"

She recognized his SUV parked at the curb. After all, it had only been a few hours since she'd hurried away from it, and him, in the lot at Kimmie's school. He'd said he wanted to talk, but she couldn't bear to hear him say good-bye. Her pulse skipped as she pulled into the driveway.

After the car had stopped, it only took Kimmie seconds to unbuckle herself and hop out. Abby took her time, trying to brace herself, shore up her defenses. She couldn't take much more of this emotional stuff. Force of habit made her press the automatic garage door opener. Then she went to see what was going on.

"This is the tent I slept in when we went camping," Kimmie boasted to three children gathered around who lived next door.

"That's right," Riley confirmed.

"Is it heavy?" four-year-old Gavin asked.

"A big guy like you wouldn't have any trouble carrying it," Riley said, and the towheaded little boy grinned at the praise.

"Girls can carry stuff, too," his seven-year-old sister Mary pointed out. Her hair was the same shade as her two brothers'. "Kimmie carried it and she's younger than me. Right, Kim?"

"Riley carried it all the way to where we camped. But I picked it up."

"No way." Colin was ten and in the boys-are-bigger-and-stronger stage. "It's too big for a girl."

"Did too, didn't I, Riley?"

"You did. When we were breaking camp, you were a big help. When you go camping, everyone has to pull his weight. That's what survival is all about." He looked at Abby as she joined the group, but his expression was as maddeningly impassive as ever.

"Hi, Mrs. Walsh," all the kids said together.

"Hi," she answered.

"Are you going camping again?" Gavin asked Riley, eyeing the tent with undisguised envy.

"Are we?" Kimmie asked.

"We'll see."

He looked at all the children who stared back with hero worship written all over their sweet, innocent faces. Abby didn't blame them. She had a raging case of it herself. Riley was definitely hero material. Although she didn't think it was especially heroic of him to show up and put her through more heartache.

"Kids, I think I hear your mother calling you," Abby said.

Colin listened. "I don't hear anything."

"I think you just got your marching orders," Riley pointed out.

"Yeah. I guess it's about time for dinner." He looked at Riley. "Can we play in the tent after we eat?"

"That's up to Mrs. Walsh," he said, meeting her gaze. Looking into his blue eyes, Abby suddenly knew what it would feel like if fire sucked all the oxygen from the air. "It's fine with me."

"Okay, let's go eat," the oldest sibling said to the other two.

When they'd gone, Abby looked at her daughter. "Kimmie, you need to go inside and wash up."

"But I'm not eatin' yet. *My* dinner's not done. Can Riley stay?"

She looked at him. "Help me out here," she pleaded.

He looked down at the little girl. "I need to talk to your mom for a few minutes. Then we'll see about dinner."

"Okay." Kim raced into the house through the open garage door.

Suddenly they were alone, and Abby didn't know what to say. He was so close she could feel the heat from his body as his breath stirred her hair. How she wanted to lean into his strength, but she didn't dare. She decided to say the obvious. "What are you doing here? What's with the tent?"

"It's about survival," he said.

"What about it? Although I have to say I'm all in favor of it."

"Me, too."

"But, Riley, I thought I made myself clear—"

"Crystal," he interrupted. "Which is why I brought the tent."

She shook her head. "You lost me."

"I hope that's not true," he said. His expression grew intense and became the one he assumed when he was on a mission and failure wasn't an option.

"When you skipped Kimmie's badge ceremony, you sent a clear message."

"Yeah. That I'm an idiot." He rubbed the back of his neck. "I'm here to get the message straight."

"By setting up the tent?"

"Today you said when camping was finished, so were we. That's unacceptable so I set up camp on your doorstep."

Abby could hardly breathe, what with the hope that expanded inside her like a helium balloon. "But, I don't understand—"

"It's about survival," he said again. "I'm prepared to camp out here indefinitely because I don't want us to be finished. I can't survive without you."

"Oh, Riley—" Her throat closed with emotion.

He curled his fingers around her upper arms and stared into her eyes. "There's a saying in the military. It's a motto that men in combat live by. Leave no man behind. That includes women and children, too."

Abby didn't say anything. She couldn't since emotion closed her throat.

"I'm completely defenseless," he said. "You and your six-year-old secret weapon have taken over my heart." He waited several moments, then frowned. "Say something, Abby."

She wanted so badly to believe what he was telling

her. Sincerity was written all over his face. But how could it not be? He was one of the good guys who took responsibility for the whole world. The same one who so badly wanted a family to belong to.

"How do I know Kimmie and I aren't substitutes for the family you lost?" she finally managed to ask.

He let out a long breath as he ran his fingers through his hair. "I don't know what I can say to convince you. Except these days, there are lots of single moms looking for a man."

Abby knew this firsthand. Many of her high school students came from single-parent homes. "What's your point?"

"If I wanted a substitute, there are lots to choose from and anyone would do. But you're not just anyone, Abby. You're—everything."

"Oh, Riley—" The lump in her throat choked off the words.

"You're right about the fact that I want a family. I found out how much when I lost mine. But you made me realize that love is the glue that keeps families together. It's the foundation everything is built on. I didn't have that the first time, and I'd rather be alone than botch things up again. In fact, I didn't even want to try, because I was afraid of making another mistake. But from the very first time I saw you, in my gut I knew that you were different and I was in trouble."

How could she resist that? As she'd said, he was the kind of man who made a girl want to try again. Finally, her heart and her head were in sync and sending a clear message all the way to her soul. Riley Dixon wasn't a chance; he was a sure thing.

"Really?" she asked.

"Really." The corners of his mouth curved up in a smile as he pulled her to him. "I love you, Abigail Walsh."

"Them's fightin' words."

He leaned back to look in her eyes. "What?"

"Never call me that. Abby will do."

"Abby will do nicely."

"I love you, too, Riley Dixon." She met his gaze and sighed. The worry and stress and pain and loneliness slipped away. "The two of us are a piece of work, you know?"

"Why's that?"

"We've been so busy protecting ourselves and everyone else, we forgot to simply love each other."

"Protection is what soldiers do. And I plan to protect you and Kimmie for as long as I live. But I won't forget to love both of you with all my heart."

"And how do I know you mean that, soldier?"

"Because I intend to marry you."

"Is that an order?"

"It could be. But I'd rather have a willing volunteer," he said.

"Ready, willing and so very able."

He smiled, then dipped his head and touched his lips to hers. As he took her weight against him, Abby savored his strength and the sensation of support. She was going to love leaning on him. She was going to love loving him.

He broke the kiss and rested his forehead to hers. "So that's a definite affirmative? You'll marry me?"

"Yes. With pleasure. And you certainly don't waste any time."

"What can I say? Once a man of action, always a man of action. There's no point in wasting any more time than we already have. This mission is on course, and there's every indication it will be a rousing success."

"So you knew I was different. In your office that first time we met," Abby said skeptically.

"Yeah. Why?"

"The way you acted, for one thing. You told me no," she reminded him.

"I'm saying yes now. In fact, I don't think I could ever say no to you again. It scares me how much I need you. How much I love you."

Her heart was overflowing with happiness and love. "But you're not afraid of anything."

"I didn't used to be. A man who's got nothing to lose has no fear. But now I've got the whole world, right here in my arms."

"Me, too." She snuggled against him, right there in front of God and all the neighbors.

She didn't care who saw that her soldier was going to make a married woman out of one very happy single mom.

* * * * *

Look for Molly's story,
IN GOOD COMPANY
available March 2006!
Only from Teresa Southwick and
Silhouette Romance.

If you enjoyed what you just read,
then we've got an offer you can't resist!

Take 2 bestselling love stories FREE!

Plus get a FREE surprise gift!

Clip this page and mail it to Silhouette Reader Service™

IN U.S.A.	IN CANADA
3010 Walden Ave.	P.O. Box 609
P.O. Box 1867	Fort Erie, Ontario
Buffalo, N.Y. 14240-1867	L2A 5X3

YES! Please send me 2 free Silhouette Romance® novels and my free surprise gift. After receiving them, if I don't wish to receive anymore, I can return the shipping statement marked cancel. If I don't cancel, I will receive 4 brand-new novels every month, before they're available in stores! In the U.S.A., bill me at the bargain price of $3.57 plus 25¢ shipping and handling per book and applicable sales tax, if any*. In Canada, bill me at the bargain price of $4.05 plus 25¢ shipping and handling per book and applicable taxes**. That's the complete price and a savings of at least 10% off the cover prices—what a great deal! I understand that accepting the 2 free books and gift places me under no obligation ever to buy any books. I can always return a shipment and cancel at any time. Even if I never buy another book from Silhouette, the 2 free books and gift are mine to keep forever.

210 SDN DZ7L
310 SDN DZ7M

Name	(PLEASE PRINT)
Address	Apt.#
City	State/Prov.	Zip/Postal Code

Not valid to current Silhouette Romance® subscribers.

Want to try two free books from another series?
Call 1-800-873-8635 or visit www.morefreebooks.com.

* Terms and prices subject to change without notice. Sales tax applicable in N.Y.
** Canadian residents will be charged applicable provincial taxes and GST.
All orders subject to approval. Offer limited to one per household.
® are registered trademarks owned and used by the trademark owner and or its licensee.

SROM04R   ©2004 Harlequin Enterprises Limited

COMING NEXT MONTH

#1802 DOMESTICATING LUC—Sandra Paul
PerPETually Yours

Puppy's got his work cut out for him when he meets his new owner, Luc Tagliano. Though grieving his lost mistress, Puppy wants this thickheaded human to see how good regular playdates with kind and patient animal trainer Julie Jones could be....

#1803 HONEYMOON HUNT—Judy Christenberry

When he hears that his wealthy father is globe-trotting with some new bride, Nick Rampling senses a gold digger's snare and teams up with Julia Chance, the bride's prim daughter. But their cat-and-mouse hunt for the couple soon convinces him it's *their* hearts that are in flight!

#1804 A DASH OF ROMANCE—Elizabeth Harbison

Run out of her catering gig by an evil queen of a boss, Rose Tilden relocates to a neighborhood Brooklyn diner. But when the handsome developer Warren Harker shows interest in the area, she learns that even the chaotic stirrings of love can create intoxicating flavors....

#1805 LONE STAR MARINE—Cathie Linz
Men of Honor

How could ex-marine captain Tom Kozlowski mistake her for a stripper-gram? Feisty schoolteacher Callie Murphy's anger cools when she sees the pain in his eyes. And as she reaches out to this wounded warrior, she's soon wondering if he can't teach *her* something powerful about the human heart....